D1527968

ROLE OF CONFLICT

APEX ACADEMY
BOOK 1

ETHAN SHAW

This is a work of fiction.

Any and all similarities to real people, places, or events are entirely coincidental.

Apex Academy Book 1 First edition. June 15, 2023

Written by Ethan Shaw

❀ Created with Vellum

LYCAON'S CURSE

...Terror struck
he took to flight, and on the silent plains
is howling in his vain attempts to speak;
he raves and rages and his greedy jaws,
desiring their accustomed slaughter, turn
against the sheep—still eager for their blood.
His vesture separates in shaggy hair,
his arms are changed to legs; and as a wolf
he has the same grey locks, the same hard face the same
bright eyes, the same ferocious look.

- *Ovid's Metamorphosis*

Log On?

The two words flashed over the computer screen. I leaned forward, bracing one hand on the narrow strip of desk between the chair and the keyboard, absently clicking YES with the other hand. The screen flashed black, and then the bright, sprawling map of Azenar appeared on the screen. It was a slow load up, but I didn't mind waiting. It had been a long day; I had two classes today, back-to-back, and even though I knew that it was an honor to be able to attend such a prestigious university... I was still damn glad to be home.

The map finally loaded in, revealing my character. I had been playing this game for almost four years now and had managed to become one of the highest-ranking players in the game. My character was a Blood Cult Barbarian class, with leather armor that had been blessed by a goddess in a hard-to-reach land. The armor was one of the best in the land and had been stained crimson from battle.

A PM came up. I clicked on it.

>Shadowclaw! Great to see you!

It was from a user named Pendragon. The corner of my mouth twitched up at the edges. I had been talking with Pendragon for a while now, and we had even teamed up against some of the newer campaigns that the game released.

I typed back: I only have about ten minutes, I'm going to hit up the spring and then run.

The spring was a magical contraption that could be visited once every twelve hours and would bestow your character with something amazing. It was usually just a high amount of krini, the in-game currency, but sometimes it would be a new level, better stats, or something of that sort. I'd once been able to get a hundred dollar's worth of cash-for-currency items, and I knew that if you were lucky enough, the goddess of the spring would bless you with a quest that could only be received through her. Four years, and I had not only never gotten it myself, but I didn't know anyone that had.

Pendragon: That's cool. I just got a ticket for the rock giant quest, we should tackle it together later.

I typed back: Will do.

The PM closed out, and I was quick to move my character through the map and to the spring in question. The graphics were great, especially for an MMORPG like this. Stepping into the fountain, my character was surrounded by a white light as the goddess gave out her blessing.

It was just krini.

Damn.

Well, ten minutes wasn't enough to start a quest, but it was enough time for me to start setting up a raid. I could log back on tomorrow and just activate it, once everything had been set up. I was in the middle of sending the raid invite to a few of my online friends, including Pendragon, and a girl named Halifax, when a different notification came through. It wasn't for the game, so I set my character to auto-train and then clicked out of the browser and into the email.

It was a new message, from somewhere called Apex Academy.

Is that a game that I had made an account with and never followed through playing?

I did that a lot, signing up whenever a new one came out and then never bothering to go back after the alpha trial ended. My tongue scraped against my top teeth. I couldn't remember anything with that name.

I clicked it. It brought up an email, quite wordy in length, with a strange crest at the top. The crest itself was a shield, with several animals attached to it. A wolf head at the top, with the shield broken into four squares, each of which contained another animal. There was a lynx, a bear, and a lizard. Beneath the shield was a banner, which read something in Latin. I didn't recognize the phrase, but it probably had something to do with learning or working together. It looked like the crest that most colleges in this part of the world liked to use, complete with the gold overlay to the black image.

I checked the address it had been sent from again. Apex Academy, huh? Alright, I would give it enough time to read.

∼

Dear Shifter

On behalf of the Apex Academy, I am happy to welcome you to our ranks. Our school is one of the most exclusive in the country, and we only accept the best students into our program. Only a small amount of alphas are discovered each year, and even fewer of them are accepted into schools. We have reached out to you, as we believe that you will make an exceptional student, and we see the potential you have in becoming a top class alpha.

Currently, you have no accolades to your name. We are certain that you will be able to swiftly attain them. Not only will you be valuable to the school and the House that it represents, you will also find that we are an incredible asset to you as well. We can offer you lessons, tools, and camaraderie.

Though our claims may seem high, we can assure you, we hold all those on our staff to the highest order. We only offer lessons that will help you better deal with the challenges you face.

To complete the enrollment process, you are required to submit the class of your shift. Please include any experience you have that might boost your ranking within the Academy. Please include a listing of family members capable of performing a shift.

If you are unfamiliar with the terms used in this message, please call the number listed below. The professors at Apex Academy are happy to answer any questions you might have. They are here to ensure that your time is spent wisely.

We are excited to have you as a student at our school. Your life as an alpha is about to become easier than ever. We hope to hear back from you shortly.

Sincerely, Dean Jason Burbank

~

What the hell kind of an email was that? There really was a phone number at the bottom of the message, but I've got no doubts that the first thing they'll do on the other side is try to get me to put my phone number in. I mean, there couldn't have been a more obvious fake email. Though I had to give them credit for the format. It sure did sound official.

I scrolled back up to the top, ready to read over it a second time when the sound of a loud bass guitar drifted through the bedroom door, followed by the riff of an electric guitar. Great. It sounded like there was about to be another raging party downstairs. I lived with a guy named Paul; we were splitting the rent because that was about the only way you could afford a house out in this part of the city. The problem was, he was a major douche. I mean, a frat boy of the highest order.

The music was cranked up even louder. I could see headlights pulling into the drive outside of the bedroom window and gave a heavy sigh, shutting the game off completely. I gave the email one last doleful look before clicking the exit button on that, too. This party was going to be headache enough, I didn't need to deal with a scam tonight, too.

Irritated, I stood up and stretched. My back was killing me. I had spent all day sitting in an uncomfortable chair at school, and now I was back home and couldn't even go stretch out on the couch. A hot shower seemed like the only alternative, and I swept quickly through my room to grab a pair of sweats and an old, soft fabric T-shirt. The logo was from an alien movie I was a fan of, though it had started fading ages ago.

Clothes in hand, I made my way to the little partial bathroom attached to my room. There was a larger, master bathroom downstairs and I was allowed to use it. There just was no way I was going to get a shower with a bunch of people over. I would just deal with the little standing shower in my six foot by six foot, standing room only bathroom.

The water in the pipes rattled when I flicked it on. It came out with a gush, a crash of water against porcelain. For some reason, I couldn't stop thinking about that scam email. It was the crest at the top of the message that caught my attention, I think. There had just been so much detail in it, it seemed... Strange to do that for a scam.

Whatever. Out of sight, out of mind, right?

2

When I got out of my shower, hair still dripping wet and leaving dark stains on the back of my t-shirt, I had three more messages waiting for me, all of them in my email. I stepped over to the computer, leaning around the side of my high-backed gaming chair to hit the open button without sitting down. The party downstairs was in full swing now, the music and the sound of people laughing and shouting drifting through the closed door.

Three emails, and they all had Apex Academy in the title of the message. I frowned, running a hand through my hair, pushing it out of my face. Water dripped down the curve of my neck, and I had to wipe the dampness off my palm before grabbing the mouse again. I was in the middle of selecting all three emails to move them to the trash when a fourth email came through.

It was from a different address, and it didn't have any topic in the line. I hovered my mouse over the top of it, debating on whether I should click it or not. After a few moments of thinking about it, I decided against it and pulled away from the computer entirely.

There was no way that I was going to fall for a scam like that – and no way that it was anything more than a scam. What did these people think I was, stupid? They either hadn't targeted their audience very well, or they had just done a bad job trying to put something together.

Even if the first email had caught my attention, the back-to-back messaging made it pretty obvious that this was just a scam.

I did pull up the original email a second time and glance it over again, my upper lip curling back with irritation as I read over the text a second time. It had a professional header and picked on all the right words. Whoever made this up must have studied acceptance letters. But there were too many weird things thrown into the paper that made it clear this was some sort of a scam.

Shifters? What does that even mean? It wasn't the only part of the email that seemed off, but it was the part that jumped out as the most obviously ridiculous. I couldn't understand why someone would go through the effort of writing this up, and then toss in something like that.

God damn, there's no way that this isn't a scam.

I just didn't understand who it was supposed to be directed at. Teenagers that were just heading out of high school, and looking to snap up a position at any academy that made them sound special?

I just didn't get it.

Clearly, in the second email they were going to talk about the registration fees and how much everything was going to cost. It was just an attempt at wringing some cash out of people that didn't know any better.

Frustrated, I pulled away from the computer, shoved my phone into the deep side pocket of my sweats, and decided to brave the party.

I wanted a drink, sue me.

Now, I wasn't a big drinker. There was just something about my nerves that were unsettled. A cold beer sounded like the best thing in the world. Maybe I could use it to wash away some of the irritation that was clinging to me.

Stepping out into the hallway, I was instantly assaulted by the full force of the music that Paul had turned on. It was some EDM nonsense that he played to make it seem more like a rave instead of an over-the-top beer party with a bunch of his frat boy friends. Someone had turned the TV on too, and it was blaring a football game of all things out of the speakers at top volume. I was hit, almost instantly, with one of the worst migraines that I had ever had.

It felt like something was trying to split my skull open, just out of nowhere. I rubbed my head.

Maybe this wasn't going to make me less irritated after all. Another spike of pressure shot through me. Yeah, I needed to grab my drink and get back to my room before the headache got bad enough that I puked, too. And damn, there was something heavy smelling in the air, too. Had they lit a whole package of incense or something?

It was like eight different colognes and aftershaves had been thrown onto the floor and just left there. Gross.

Making my way out into the living room, I found that the lights were harsh on my eyes, too; that the whole world seemed a little too bright. It must have been from the migraine. I blinked hard, scrubbing at my face with the meat of one palm and then making my way into the kitchen. The house itself was modern, but Paul had really messed it up over the year that we had been living together. He'd slapped this ugly bright purple paint on the wall, and all the furniture was a mismatched mess that he had gotten from this friend or that friend, most of it either stained or sporting cigarette burns.

The kitchen counters were piled full of beer cans and red solo cups already, which meant that this party was going to last all night. I was planning on grabbing a beer for myself, but now that the headache had grabbed me, I figured it was safer to stick with one of the sports drinks in the fridge.

I grabbed one of them, cracking it open and guzzling half of the drink standing there in the kitchen. It was way too sweet, but I kept them on hand for after my midnight runs. Half the bottle gone, I turned, scanning the crowd. There was Randy Ashton, and Carly Emmers, and even the twins, Frankie and Freddie Batson, had shown up.

Yeah.

This party was a hard pass for me.

I headed back towards my room. Gary Kravin stumbled backward, shoulder checking me. Sports drink splashed onto the floor and the front of my shirt. "Seriously?"

Anger shot through me, an irrational amount. Gary spun around and shoved me. "Watch it, asshole!"

The guy was clearly wasted, red in the face, and hazy-eyed. I should have just left. I normally would have. But the migraine spiked and my bad mood got even worse. I shoved him back and said, "You're the one who ran into me, jackass. Try thinking shit through before you start running your mouth."

"You little-" Gary threw his beer. Half-warm Pabst splashed over my chest. Something in the back of my head snapped, just like that. With a furious sound, I threw myself forward and tackled him. I could feel heat racing through my body

Gary hit the ground, and I went down on top of him. I

brought my fist back and slammed it into his face as hard as I could, my knuckles aching at the impact. Gary rolled us easily and got me in the chest. It knocked the air from my lungs. The heat in my skin was unbearable. It felt like I was on fire. A rabid snarl tore uncontrollably from the back of my throat. I made this awful sound in the back of my throat, like a rabid dog snarling at someone that had come too close.

Something was wrong.

I was wrong.

The change wracked through my body, twisting my form. My muscles grew hot and then they expanded, sixty pounds of it suddenly clinging to my form. With another roar, I flung Gary backward. He went flying off of me and halfway across the room, slamming into the coffee table and sending beer bottles scattering in all directions.

People were suddenly looking at us. Frankie ran over and helped Gary up. "What the hell, Gary?"

"That little shit!" There was blood dripping from the corner of Gary's mouth. He spat on the ground, and then pulled himself up and charged at me again. I was moving on instincts that I didn't understand, pulling myself up onto my feet and meeting him head-on. My whole view of the room had shifted, as though I had grown by several inches. My fist slammed into Gary's side, and my other hand grabbed him by the back of the neck. As soon as he staggered, I grabbed onto his hair with my second hand and used the grip to slam his head down into my knee.

Crunch.

Gary's nose broke against my knee. Blood gushed onto my sweatpants, which no longer fit me the way that they should. Frankie grabbed me from behind, throwing me down onto the ground and bringing his boot-clad foot down into the center of my stomach. I grunted, grabbing onto his ankle with both hands.

My nails, suddenly sharper than before, raked over his skin. I managed to pull his leg out from under him, bringing one fist down onto his crotch and then throwing myself around to catch Gary in the jaw before he could jump me from behind. I slammed my fist into his jaw so hard that it gave a sickening wet pop, crunching beneath the force of my hit.

The tang of blood was sweet in my nose; the way that it gushed into his mouth where he bit his tongue, the way that it ran down from his broken nose. Gary went down howling, grabbing at his face with both hands, fingers digging into skin that was already starting to purple with bruising and swelling.

Paul demanded to know, "What the hell are you doing?"

I went to make another swing at Frankie, who had gotten to his feet. Paul grabbed me by the wrist before I could. I spun around and shoved him hard.

Paul staggered backward, throwing his hands up in the air. "Christ, Victor! I know that they're dicks, but calm the fuck down! You're taking this way too far!"

The music had stopped. Freddie had moved to his twin's side, hands out, like he was ready to get in the way if the fight picked up again. Someone had crouched down next to Gary, who was still wailing and making those pathetic sounds. Blood was running out of his mouth. It looked like there was a tooth on the floor.

"I think we need to call 911," said the guy, already reaching for his phone. "I think his jaw's broken."

There was blood on my knuckles. Gary's blood. The migraine was fading, and with it, my anger seemed to drain away. I couldn't understand why I had done that. Or how I had done it, even. Had my body really grown larger, stronger, or had someone just spiked the sports drink and then tossed it back into the fridge? I could no longer smell the copper tang of Gary's blood, or the overpowering mixture of cologne and aftershave.

Paul shoved my shoulders, pushing me towards the door. "You need to get out of here, Victor. Go cool off!"

"Don't do that," Frankie spit. "He needs to be arrested!"

"We've got way too much shit on us," Paul said. "No one wants the cops to show up. And look, just – he's fine. You're fine. Gary started that shit anyway."

"I don't care," Frankie said, waving a hand through the air. "His jaw's broke!"

I took a step towards the door, away from the shouting. Freddie tried to convince his brother, "and he deserved it. Just calm down, Frankie. Paul's right. We don't want the cops to show up here. It's bad enough that we have to get an ambulance out here."

Frankie still didn't look like he was going to listen. I backed out of the living room, horrified that I would do something like that. I wasn't a fighter. I was the kind of guy who studied, read, and played games online. There was a spell when I was younger where I liked to consider myself a hacker, and I took midnight runs because I often found myself plagued with a restless sort of energy that kept me from sleeping. But fighting? That had never been my thing.

Even when I was in high school, I had never gotten into any brawls. I wasn't a shy kid; I just had a level head and a good grip on myself.

And that anger. It had swelled up inside of me like a wave, threatening to drown me. I hadn't been able to breathe through it. I hadn't been able to think through it. The wave had crashed down on top of me, and it had plastered me into this mode where all I could think about was beating the fuck out of Gary, and making sure that he knew I was the one in charge.

I was top dog. Not him. The thought passed through my head, only making my nerves tick up that much more. My nails had gone back to their normal length, but there was blood under them from where I had scraped my fingers over Frankie's ankle.

I hit the door, one hand reaching around behind me to grope at the handle. It gave beneath my palm, finally swinging open. Cold evening air gushed against me. Frankie and Paul were still arguing, but it sounded like someone else had already gotten on the phone with the cops, giving out the address of the house and some vague information about a drunken fight at a party.

My name wasn't dropped, but I knew that if I was still around here when the EMTs showed up, Frankie was going to rat me out. That was just the kind of guy he was. A sore loser, a liar, and a cheat.

So – I had to make sure that I wasn't around. With any luck, Paul would be able to smooth things over without me and I wouldn't get in too much trouble.

I turned, darting outside, into the twilight heavy sky, and I ran.

It was early morning before I came back to the house. Streaks of dusty yellow still stained the sky, and the yard was pretty much ruined. It always looked like this after one of Paul's parties. The guy let things get out of hand. It was mostly because Paul hung around with people like the twins and Gary. The door wasn't locked, which meant that I hadn't been kicked out after the fight.

The inside of the house was in pretty much the same state. The ambulance coming out must not have killed the party. There were red solo cups and empty beer cans all around the living room and pretty much coating the kitchen counter. A few empty pizza boxes took up the center of the coffee table, and everything that *had* been on it had just been pushed aside, knocked onto the floor.

I didn't want to actually speak to anyone just yet... But I was starving. Like, it seriously felt like I hadn't eaten in weeks. I went into the kitchen, pulling open the door to the fridge. There was a wrapped up burger sitting on one of the shelves, leftover from a fast food run a few days ago. It was

Paul's, but I grabbed it and ate it anyway. Way too much mustard for my taste. It didn't make me feel any better.

A quick scan of the fridge, and I found a container of leftover spaghetti and meatballs. I devoured it. Standing right there in the open doorway like some kind of a freak, using my fingers to pull the noodles and the sauce covered meatballs out of the container and shove them in my mouth. The meat was the best part. Even though they were just store-bought things from the freezer section, it still was like I was dining on the best slice of sirloin steak.

The container got tossed into the sink to wash later. I licked the sauce off of each finger, and then my lower lip. Why was I still so hungry? It was like whatever had happened the night before, it had done something to my physiology. I couldn't get enough to eat.

But I also didn't want to get caught down there eating everything in the fridge when Paul showed up. I grabbed a chunk of white bread from the loaf, slathered it in peanut butter, and took it to my room with me. There wasn't a lock on the door, or I would have clicked it. I just wanted to be alone.

The peanut butter caked against my back molars. Were they sharper than they should be? It felt like they might have changed shape, and when I ran my tongue over my front teeth, I was met with that same sensation. Not knife sharp, but pointed enough that it scraped over the flat of my tongue.

What was that last night? I had spent hours trying to figure it out, but kept coming up with a blank spot. The most I could come up with was that my anger had some kind of physical reaction. It had cut into me, it had twisted me, making me into something else entirely.

A beat of rage pulsed through me. I remembered that

much. Being so angry that it almost hurt. And my body –
had it just been in my head, the way that my muscles had
grown in size, the way that I had gotten taller? If it was, well,
then I had been drinking something totally spiked. But my
body ached in a way that made me think it must have actually happened. In a way that made me wonder if I had really
been bigger before.

That would be why I was starving, right? My body had
gone through some sort of growth spurt.

"God, that's so stupid." I groaned and dropped backward onto the bed. The mattress creaked beneath me
when I flopped onto it, leaving one leg hanging off of the
edge. "I didn't grow, just because I got pissed off. I'm not
the Hulk."

Saying it out loud, that made me sound even more child-
ish. I just couldn't seem to come up with another explanation. Twenty-three years old, and I had gotten into my first
fight. I had broken the jaw of someone twice my size and
three years older than me.

Hands pressed against my face, dragging down over my
cheeks. I rolled onto my side. What I really needed to do
right then was just clear my head. And considering I had
been up all night pacing through the city and trying to
figure out what was going on, taking a nap seemed like the
best way to do that. Afterward, I would get a shower and
then... then things would make sense.

I just needed to rest.

Laying down didn't get me anywhere. I was too restless
for that. My mind kept drifting back to the fight the night
before. The way it had felt when bone snapped beneath my
knuckles. The way that the adrenaline from the fight had
rushed through me, better than any high I had ever been on.
The scent of Gary's blood. The way that my hand had ached

afterward, though the bruising had already cleared up by the morning.

Going to sleep clearly wasn't on the table. I needed to try and come up with something else instead. Getting off of the bed, I went over to the computer desk. My first instinct was to get online and start up a raid for a real distraction, but... Then I remembered the email that I had gotten.

Everything got weird then. What had it said? That I was part of the Apex Academy. It talked about shifting forms and alphas, too. The concept had been absolutely laughable when the email came through. On some level, it still was.

All the same, a part of me couldn't help but wonder if it actually had something to do with the weird shit that had happened yesterday. I was grasping at straws, and I knew it, but I didn't have any other leads. I mean, something had to cause that, right? I wouldn't have just broken that kid's jaw if I wasn't being affected by something.

Maybe it was some sort of hypnosis, something that had a code word in it to activate – God, no. I cut that train of thought off right away. That was just stupid. All the same, I started logging into my email. This had to be where I started. If nothing popped out at me while I was reading the email... I could go from there.

But no sooner had I pulled up the email than a hand was banging on the closed bedroom door. Paul's voice demanded, "Come on, Victor. Open up. You've got a visitor."

Fear shot through me. Had the cops been waiting for me to show up at the house so they could interview me? I figured that I was in a lot of trouble. For a moment, I debated on just not getting up and opening the door... but they wouldn't be here if Paul wasn't certain I was home. The containers in the sink had given me away.

So, I rolled onto my feet, standing up and shuffling over

to the door. I used the front of one hand to try and smooth the wrinkles out of my shirt and push down the cowlicks of my hair, just in case it really was a cop. Then I put on my best face and opened the door. "What?"

Paul stood there next to an older man. He had to be in his fifties, maybe even closer to his sixties. Though I was certain that I had never seen the man before in my life, there was something about him that seemed familiar. The scent of cedar wood incense clung to his skin and underneath it, there was something else. Something that he recognized.

Paul looked super unhappy to be there. "I guess you were right. He is home."

"I told you," said the man. He stepped into the room, glancing over it. The man wore a heavy, rust red colored canvas jacket, and a pair of denim jeans that had clearly seen better days. A cane, carved into the shape of a bear at the top, was clutched in one hand. In the other hand, he held a single letter. The envelope had my name on the front and had been stamped with a wax seal matching the crest of the ridiculous emails I had gotten the night before.

I looked over my shoulder. The email for Apex Academy had finished loading and was sitting on the main display screen of my desktop. I had a secondary screen sitting on the side but hadn't bothered to turn the monitor on this morning. There wouldn't have been any need for it.

"Victor Rawlings," said the man, a note of pride curling through his words. He held out one hand. "It's been a very long time since I saw you last. I'm honored to meet you now, though."

I took his hand, surprised by how strong his grip was – and how many callouses were on the bottom of his palm, too. In fact, the callouses really caught me by surprise. "Sorry. I don't... know who you are?"

Paul shrugged. "He threw a fit at the door. I tried to tell him that you were sick or whatever and didn't want visitors, but he said-"

"That was inane, and I already knew what was wrong with you," the man said. "I'm not an idiot. I could tell that it would happen soon, and the moment that I got to the front door, I could smell the traces of the Primal Shift, still clinging to the air."

"The what?" I asked, frowning. I pulled my hand back and shook my head. "No, wait. Let's put a pause on that and back up some. Who are you?"

"My name is Aaron," said the man. "And I'm your uncle."

I stared at him. "My uncle?"

As far as I was aware, I didn't actually have any family. Not living. My mother passed away when I was a lot younger, and she claimed that my father had been dead for years.

Aaron continued, "Your father was my younger brother. I thought that when he passed on... But – ah, that doesn't matter right now. In the list of things that you and I need to discuss, our family history is down at the bottom."

A frown curled over my features. I was on edge still after the night before, and I didn't like the way that this guy was dismissing my questions.

"Maybe for you, but I don't remember my mother ever talking about my father having a brother," I told him, sharply. "And I don't know that there's any reason to trust you."

Aaron's mouth twisted up, the expression hauntingly familiar. He reached into his coat pocket and said, "I thought that you might throw a fit over this. Here. Make it a quick fit."

The man pulled his wallet out. From it, he pulled a picture. It had clearly just been brought along for my benefit. I could tell that he wasn't the sort to be sentimental enough to carry around photographs. The picture was of my father and another boy. I imagined it must have been Aaron. They were younger, only a year or so older than me, and they wore university uniforms. The dark blue blazers made them both look sharp as could be.

"I know that you never knew about me," said Aaron. "But that was for your own safety, not because I did something wrong. If I'd had a choice in it, I would've seen you years ago."

There was a crest on each of their blazer pockets. The same crest from the letter that Aaron was holding. The same crest from the top of the email. Apex Academy.

Anger started to twist in the back of my chest. I wasn't sure if this guy was actually my uncle or not, but it was clear that he knew what was going on. At first, I thought that the Academy had just been some kind of mass email scam. But now that the crest was showing up elsewhere, I knew that it had to be a lot more than that.

And Aaron knew all about it.

I took a step towards him. A low growl slipped out through my teeth, the sound startling me. Paul stared, open-mouthed. "Dude, what the fuck is going on with you?"

I realized that I didn't have an answer for Paul. I had no idea where all this anger was coming from, and I sure as hell didn't understand why I was growling and baring my teeth, like some sort of fucked up, pissed off dog. It was just like the night before. Aaron barely had to speak to me, and I was already looking to throw down.

Just the thought of possibly getting into a fight had been enough to make my fingers ball up into fists at my side. I could have easily taken a swing at Aaron and been totally fine with it.

I might have, if it hadn't been for Paul standing there.

Aaron, on the other hand, looked like he had been waiting for this exact moment. He reached out, putting a hand on Paul's shoulder and turning him back towards the door. Once Paul had been herded into the hallway, Aaron grabbed the handle of the door.

"Sorry kid," he said, tugging the door shut. "This conversation... Is private."

Click. The door was pushed shut.

And just like that, we were alone.

4

The car raced down the interstate, nothing on either side of us but trees, fields, and the occasional billboard. I wasn't totally positive how I had been convinced to come out here with Aaron. It was a long way from where I had been attending law school. Longer still from where I had actually been raised.

The guy's family home was outside of the main city of New York, in the rural stretch of the state. He lived somewhere between an old quarry and a huge pinewood forest. We had already been in the car for what felt like ages, even though it was closer to only having been twenty minutes.

We hadn't been talking since we left. Aaron said that if I came out to the house with him for the weekend, he would explain everything. I figured that it was a better option than killing Paul because he ate the last of the pizza or something. With the way my temper had been flaring up, I was seriously concerned that might have happened. And I would have been way less content breaking my friend's jaw than I was with breaking Gary's.

The car tires caught on a dip in the road and the whole

vehicle rocked. I snapped a hand out, steadying the open can of Red Bull in the cup holder next to me. The sugar-filled liquid splashed up onto my palm.

"Not much longer," said Aaron, breaking the tense silence that had fallen over us. I frowned a little, not sure what to say in response. I had questions, of course, but Aaron had made it clear that we wouldn't be going over any of them until we got to his house.

"Okay," I told him, with a heavy sigh. "Didn't realize that you lived all the way out here."

"Never lived in the city," said Aaron.

"Never?"

"No."

I asked, "What about my father?"

At the mention of the man, Aaron's mouth pulled into a tight line. There was something like grief in his gaze, a heavy sort of anger behind it. He shook his head and tightened his grip on the steering wheel. It was obvious that I had just hit a sore spot.

The man said nothing.

I told him, "I'm going to take that as a no," and turned to look out the window again. "You realize that you aren't the only one unhappy, right?"

"You don't know the half of it," started Aaron.

I cut him off. "Yeah, I don't. I know that I went fucking psycho on someone last night and that you seem-" I made a face, barely stopping myself from calling him a prick. "Like I'm not actually going to get any answers from you."

That was probably the response that was least likely to put me out on the side of the road.

I wasn't done yet though, continuing, "and you know what? That's not going to fly with me for a whole lot longer.

You know what's going on with me and you just aren't saying shit."

Aaron glanced at me from the corner of his eyes. He made another face, nose wrinkling up like an unhappy dog.

"Nothing?" I asked. A part of me had really been hoping that was going to get something out of him.

I would have even settled for a *shut up* just to have something to push back against. The silence in the car was oppressive. Even worse was the confusion. I had only come out with Aaron because I wanted to know what was wrong with me.

I had been expecting Aaron to start spilling beans the moment that we got out on the long, straight stretch of the highway.

But no, that hadn't happened.

Even trying to push against him just got me the same dry look that I had been dealing with all day. I rolled my eyes and turned back to the window, staring at the side of the road as it rushed past. This stretch of the highway was lined with trees and fields. The fields looked overgrown, as though no one actually tended them. No cows in them, either.

My scowl deepened. The longer that the silence drug on, the worse my mood started to get.

I wasn't sure what was going on with Aaron, but I knew that there were going to be all kinds of issues if the guy didn't start giving me some answers soon.

My temper was too quick to flare up. I didn't know nearly enough about what was going on. And honestly? My mood was pretty shit. The long drive wasn't helping. A strange restlessness had been born inside of me. I wanted to get out of the car and move, to run.

It was even worse now than it had been before. The forest that I could see in the distance was calling to me.

Weird, since I had never been much of a nature guy before. I liked books, I liked studying, and I liked playing on the computer. Hiking, camping, that sort of thing – it had never been an interest to me. It looked like that might be changing. Whatever happened to me the night before, it had altered the way that I thought about things. About the whole world, it seemed.

A new strength and interest was burning inside of me. And I would find the answer to it in that forest.

The thought was unnerving. I didn't know what it meant. My own emotions seemed to be betraying me and going haywire, straight off of the deep end.

He pulled off of the main highway, onto one of the nearby exits – and then from there, onto a small, winding back road. It wasn't dirt, but you could tell that the pavement had only been put down in the last ten years. There weren't any holes in it, and the color was dark as sin still. The trees got thicker, and the road grew narrower.

This was the kind of road that most people didn't take.

The trees were plastered with NO TRESPASSING signs. Some of them were old and sun faded, and others were clearly new, recently hung up, and still bright in color. A handmade wooden sign was hammered into the ground at one point, and that one read NO TRESPASSING too, though the warning was painted on in big, black letters.

"Do you own the road?" I asked.

Aaron grunted an affirmation. "Whole lot is private property. You shouldn't ever see a truck out here but mine."

"What about when people get lost?"

"They can turn around and take their lost asses somewhere else," said Aaron, with a snort. "Otherwise, they're gonna have to deal with my dogs."

I gave him a sideways look. "You didn't seem like a dog person."

"Hope you aren't scared of hounds," Aaron said.

Even if I was, it was too late to turn back now. We both knew that.

Soon, the truck was barreling down a one lane drive, pine branches framing it on either side.

A sharp turn sent me sliding into the door. The seat belt bit into my shoulder. At the end of the bend, the main property was visible. A wide stretch of land with only a few sparse trees on it, and a big, three-story farmhouse at the end of a twisting dirt drive. There was a wraparound front porch on the building, and true to his words, two old hound dogs sitting beneath a rocking chair.

The dogs stood up as the truck pulled up in front of the building. They started barking and yapping up a storm. Aaron rolled down the window and snarled at them, this deep, throaty thing. With a whine, the two dogs laid back down.

They didn't look like the kind of dogs that would actually bother trespassers. It made me wonder if Aaron was more bark than bite. Also, that growl? Maybe the weirdest thing that I've heard a guy do.

It was impossible to forget about the fact that I had growled at Aaron earlier in the day, though. In fact, an echoing grumble was sitting in the back of my chest, as though stirred to life by the sound of Aaron fussing at his dogs.

"Christ," I muttered, under my breath. I stepped out of the car, soft grass bending underneath my sneakers. A single hastily packed bag had been thrown into the bed of the truck. It didn't have much in it. Some clothes, my laptop, a few basic essentials.

I wasn't the most sentimental person, so a quick run through the room had been pretty easy to accomplish. Everything that I didn't want, I had just left in the room. At the time, I had planned on coming back to get them.

For some reason, now that I was here, I was starting to think that probably wouldn't happen. It was like the very air on the property was trying to tell me something.

You're home, it seemed to say. *This is where you're supposed to* be.

It was actually more unnerving than it was comforting. I grabbed it out, slinging the strap of it over my shoulder. "Now what?"

"Rosie," said Aaron, nodding at the hound dog with a black saddle marking on her back. "And Daisy."

The second dog was a little lighter in color and all brown, save one patch on her hind leg. They both had big wet eyes, which they blinked up at me. I said, "cute dogs."

"Pains in the ass, that's what they are." Aaron stopped and gave each dog a scratch on the ear before vanishing into the house. I did the same as I followed him up.

"Yeah? They seem to listen pretty good," I told him.

"Only because someone else is around. They're putting on a show," Aaron said. He unlocked the front door and pushed it open. The two dogs rushed past us, nearly knocking me over in their haste to get into the house first.

Aaron didn't say anything to scold them, just gave the two dogs an irate look before stepping in after them and bidding me to follow.

The longer I was around Aaron, the more obvious it was that we really were related. Aaron had the same irritated expression that I did, and he held himself the same way, too. And he looked just like my father, but a little bit older.

The inside of the house looked just the same as the outside; it was clear that a single man lived here, and that he had a penchant for hunting. A deer mount hung on the wall above the fireplace, and a layer of dust clung to the stuffed ducks on the mantle. There was an old patchwork quilt tossed over the back of the couch, but it was faded with age and looked to be the only hint of a woman's touch in the place.

I asked, "Are you married?"

"Used to be," said Aaron. "She passed almost twenty years ago now. Couldn't bring myself to get with anyone after that." He gestured at a wall with lines of photographs on it. "She's the one in red."

I walked over to it. The woman in red was small and dainty, almost mouse-like in appearance. But there was a spark to her gaze that was impossible to ignore, a burning heat that made it clear she must have been a real firebrand of a woman. "She's pretty."

"She was beautiful," said Aaron with a sigh. "Come on, up this way."

He didn't wait for me to respond, just moving and heading towards the stairs. I lingered in the living room for a moment before following him up to the second floor, and then to the very end of the hallway. He pushed open an old, battered-looking door and let me into what must have been the guest bedroom.

The sad thing was, this place must have been gorgeous at one point. You could tell from the curls of the crown molding, the dark wood along the base of the walls, and the parquet wood floor. But no one had been taking care of it lately, and the whole place just seemed a little darker, a little older, and a little dirtier than one would expect from such an expensive family home.

The guest bedroom was the same. A king-sized bed in the middle of one room, and a big dirty bay window that overlooked the back half of the property. There was an old trunk sitting at the foot of the bed, a small wooden box on the top of it. I was drawn to the box. It had such an odd aura to it. A smell, too, something floral and familiar.

"You can stay in here," said Aaron. "It's not much, not for you, but it's going to have to do for now. I've already put in a call. I'll have someone that can take you to the Academy when it starts up in a few months."

"I never said that I was going," I told him, running my fingers over the top of the box. It was a simple thing, with the carving of a bear on the top of it. I lifted it up. Inside, there were loose photographs and a single necklace. The necklace itself was dainty, a strand of silver with an odd symbol at the base; a metal eternity sign, inlaid three times.

The back of it had my mother's initials carved into it. I ran it through my fingers, letting the chain slide through my grip.

It was strange hearing people talk about my parents, but I tried not to let anyone realize how much it unsettled me. My father was a shadowy figure in my past, forgotten but still had a strong presence. Mostly because he practically haunted my mother. She was always talking about him in one way or another.

And my mom... She got a strange illness when I first left for college. She had told me that she was going to a facility somewhere that would give her constant watch and help, but... It didn't do anything. She passed away. I didn't have anything of hers.

Not like this.

Aaron said, "I wouldn't have that shit if I was lying to you. Going to the Academy, its important. Not just for you, either. For all of us."

"How did you get this?" I asked. I only had a few memories of my mother, but in each of those, she was wearing this necklace. And in each of the photographs in the box, my mother was wearing this necklace, too.

It wasn't mine, but it should have been.

Aaron seemed to think so too as he didn't say anything to stop me as I reached up and slid it around my neck. The chain was long enough that I could tuck it into the front of my shirt, so that it wasn't visible most of the time.

"She left it here," said Aaron. "Your mother's story isn't the important one. Don't look at me like that, I'm telling you the truth. Her story isn't what matters here. What matters is that you're something special, and it's about to hit you in full force."

"The fight yesterday. You said that you knew about it." I was trying not to let my short temper get the best of me, but it was hard. I wanted to bite at something. To sink my teeth into something. It was the strangest urge. I almost didn't know how to parse through it.

I breathed out hard, Was my irritation visible on my face? It must have been. Aaron looked stupidly amused by something. By me, probably.

"Yes, I knew about it. A lot of people do. You read that email," said Aaron. "And the letter that I gave you in the car."

The letter. It had been from the Academy, with a little more information on each of the classes that were offered. Strange ones about shifting into an animal form, about alchemy.

Magic.

But magic wasn't real.

It was just something in games. Books. Movies.

"I read it," I told him. "But it sounded like a joke."

It sounded like absolute bullshit. I'm having to work really, really hard not to start something.

Aaron shook his head. "It's not. The school has been running for over two hundred years, and it's a cornerstone in our society."

"Our society. What the hell is that supposed to mean?" I demanded, shaking my head again. "My society is the one I was just in."

"No, it's not," said Aaron. "And it means that you aren't normal, and you know it. You're part of our family, Victor. That means you're a shifter. And more than that, you're the strongest that we've got," said Aaron. "There are smaller packs all over the place, but the greater packs – that's what we are. Each greater pack has one Progenitor. The Prime is not only the strongest, but has the ability to take on the many aspects of all the other shifters."

"Shifters. What, like a werewolf?" I asked. It was hard to keep up with him. The letter in the car had spoken a little bit about packs, but I hadn't taken any of it seriously. It was massively weird to look at a fully grown man like Aaron and watch him act like all of this was real.

Aaron let out a bark of laughter. "Not quite. The first Primogenitors were five brothers who offended Agnon by stealing fruit, meat, and mead from his temple. They were cursed with their affliction and dispersed across the world to live out their days. These first Primes couldn't control their urges. Those that survived their attacks shifted into the Five Aspects, which would later become known as lynx, lycan, bear kin, avian, and aurian. That's how our society started."

I wanted to argue. To say that I didn't believe him.

But this was the truth of the matter: I did believe him.

The words resonated inside of me. It gave me a physical sensation of contentedness to listen too. "You aren't joking."

"I'm not," said Aaron.

"So what, these five shifters started a whole secret society?" I questioned. It sounded stupid to say it out loud. The tips of my ears were hot with embarrassment.

Aaron said, "They thrived, having no rivals other than each other. And they broke off, eventually, into houses. Greater packs that had more power than the scattered ones. You're going to learn more about them at the Academy, but the point is, you're part of House Blackstone. You're supposed to inherit it."

"Inherit what?"

"The whole house," said Aaron. "The whole subsection of pack members in this stretch of the country."

I froze, my gaze drifting up toward my uncle. "What?"

Aaron's mouth twitched up at the corner, into the start of a smile. "There we are. That's the look I was waiting for. You can't tell me that you don't feel it. That fire burning inside of you. It was ignited yesterday, when you went through a Primal Shift. But it's still burning even now."

He was right. There was a heat in my chest, this low burning flame that I couldn't put out.

The source of my anger.

It was something else too, though. More than just irritation. It was a part of me that had been missing. A broken glass, finally glued back together.

"Fine, I believe you. I believe that I went through something yesterday." I said. "That I felt something. But what does this have to do with house-"

"House Blackstone."

"Exactly, that," I said. "What does that have to do with me?"

Aaron continued, "House Blackstone is meant to be yours. You're the prime, Victor. Set to be the strongest out of all of us. But just like they went and they culled your father, they're going to try and cull you too. You're only going to inherit the house if you can survive long enough. That's why we need to get you to the Academy."

"The prime. Like... the leader? The top dog?"

"Top dog. That's funnier than you realize." Aaron chuckled. He had a strange sense of humor, as it was turning out. "Top everything is more like it. You're meant to lead, Victor. All of us."

"What's... Blackstone?"

"What do you mean?"

"I'm a Rawlings, right?" I said. "That much wasn't a lie?"

Aaron nodded. "Blackstone, that was the name of the man that started the house, ages ago. But prime, it's not always passed down to someone in the same family. It made a jump at some point, into the Rawlings bloodline. Wouldn't do to change the name of the whole house. Would be like changing the name of the country every time there was a new President."

I asked, "So Blackstone was one of the original shifters?"

"Now you're catching on," said Aaron. "It's a lot to take in, but the classes at the Academy, they'll do a better job at explaining this kind of thing."

I should have been calling it out as bullshit, a total lie. Should have asked what the man was smoking to come to this decision. But I couldn't bring myself to say any of that. There was a part of me that just instantly knew he was correct. My uncle wasn't lying to me. I understood that on a primal level.

My gaze turned back to the pictures in the box. I shuffled through them a few times, taking in the way that my mother was smiling in all of them. The way that my father has such a serious look on his face. "Did they kill him?"

Silence greeted me. Aaron spoke with a choked voice after a few long seconds, telling me, "Your father was a good man. People say a lot of shit about him but... My brother, he had heart."

"So, that's a yes." I didn't know anything about my father. Looking at the picture before me was one of the only times I had actually seen the guy's face.

"Power is a hard thing to keep hold of," Aaron told me.

"But you want me to take it. To be in the same place he died."

"You should get some rest," said Aaron. "Take the day to look around the place, answer a few of your own questions. I don't know how to give you an answer to that, not right now at least. You've got to try and figure it out on your own."

And then the guy turned, and he left, and it was just me then, in the middle of the guest room. The light coming in through the window was darker, geared more toward the evening. It made the shadows seem that much starker and made the walls seem that much taller.

I put the pictures back into the box, setting the lid on it and putting the box itself back onto the trunk. I set my bag down on the floor at the foot of the bed and stepped over to the window. The glass was dirty and had smears over it, but it was still a decent enough view. The backside of the property jutted up against a thick stretch of the pine forest, and that forest had trees so dark, they looked like shadows themselves.

I frowned a little bit, pressing my forehead against the glass. Did it make me nuts, that I was considering believing

Aaron? Did it make me totally nuts that I was considering all this talk about people who could change into animals to be real? Maybe. But it felt like the right thing to do. It felt like the guy was being honest with me.

I wanted to believe him.

That would explain where my parents were, and it would explain what had happened yesterday too. That anger in the back of my chest, the fire that was burning, the email. It would explain all of it.

And fuck, I desperately wanted some amount of an explanation at this point.

5

"Alright." It was only ten in the morning, but Aaron had already cajoled me to go outside with him, into the back-yard. "I told you that we would start getting your answers, and we're going to do exactly. I'm going to prove to you that you'll be able to take on another form."

I nodded.

I had decided that the best thing I could do was just go along with him and see where it took me.

That being said, I would have liked to have at least gotten breakfast first. When I said as much, Aaron laughed at me. "We'll get something to eat later. Come on, kid, don't you want to see what you can do?"

"What CAN I do?" I asked him.

Aaron tilted his head back, glancing up at the bright sun above us. "You're going to be able to pull off a hell of a lot. But right now, you can learn how to fight."

"Like karate?"

"Not quite. We're going to start with something else. Something more... Fitting," Aaron said.

I didn't like the tone of voice that he was using. It made

the hair on the back of my neck stand up. I asked, "Why does that sound fun?"

Aaron asked, "What do you mean?"

"Fighting. Doing something like that," I elaborated. "Why does that sound like fun?"

Aaron shook his head. "Shouldn't it?"

"I've never liked fighting before."

"Your mom raised a strange kid, huh?"

A growl slipped between my teeth. The sound startled me back a step. I raised a hand and pressed it against my own mouth, shocked.

Aaron said, "It's the same as that sound you just made. Your natural instincts are starting to come out. You're going to be learning a lot about yourself in the next few months. I bet you're going to be finding a lot of new things that feel right, too."

Instincts.

It sounded like an asinine answer, but it also felt... Right.

That would explain why I had wanted to run off into the forest the moment that I laid eyes on it, at least. It would explain why I was so excited about getting into a fight, too, despite the fact that I normally only took my violence on the computer screen.

The way that Aaron said that though... It made me a little uneasy.

What other new instincts were going to be cropping up in the coming days? The coming months, in his own words. My brows furrowed.

Aaron clapped his hands together. The shock of sound snapped my attention back to him. "Get lost in thought some other time, kid. We've got work to do today."

"I wasn't lost in thought," I grumbled, but I did turn my full attention back onto the man, just as had been requested.

Aaron took on a stance outside, spreading his legs apart. He pressed a hand to his chest. "You're going to focus on the fire in your heart. Think about it growing and building. Let it take over you. It will happen naturally, meant to change in due course. Your body and your spirit know the form that it's supposed to take."

"Right." I nodded and took a deep breath, mirroring the broad stance that my uncle had adopted. I closed my eyes and tried to focus on the heat that was building up in my chest. It was quickly all consuming, easy to understand what my uncle meant. Just like in the fight two nights ago, it turned into something else, twisting inside of my chest and then pushing outwards. I could feel the difference in my body, the way that my muscles twisted and bulged.

It somehow happened in a matter of seconds, and yet it seemed to take an eon. The heat pushed outwards, and my body seemed to explode into a different shape. I was no longer trapped in human form. Rather, I was a bear. My body was incredibly tall and broad, covered in thick black fur with massive, clawed paws. I appeared to be similar to a real bear but with a human's ability to walk upright. My mouth hung open, and I let out a guttural snarl.

The heat was still there. It burned beneath my skin like a fever. I tried to hold onto it, but the shift was too much, and I collapsed back onto my own human legs before even sixty seconds had passed. They gave out beneath me, and my uncle began to clap and laugh, cheering me on.

"That's it! That's what I knew would happen," said Aaron.

I spat, and the slime was tinged with red. One of my teeth was bleeding around the gums. It felt like my limbs had just been turned into jelly. I could barely force myself into a sitting position, let alone stand up. "What was that?"

A fierce hunger slammed into me. It felt like I had been starving myself for weeks. I curled my arms around myself. My stomach gave an audible growl. I was really, really regretting not getting breakfast before coming out here now.

Aaron told me, "That was proof that you are going to be exactly what House Blackstone needs. The bear kin are one of the strongest shifts. In that form, you're going to be a total killing machine." He took a knee in front of me, clapping a big hand on my shoulder. "You're going to have a hard time learning to control yourself, but I have faith in you."

"Bear kin," I echoed.

Aaron nodded. "The lack of control makes bear kin more susceptible to injury. They are all offense, no defense, but their bodies are very tough and hard to kill. And you're not just a bear kin. That's the thing, Victor. You're the prime alpha. Starting as a bear kin, that's going to mean you're the host to great power."

"I still don't get it," I groaned. "The prime alpha? What, like in a wolf pack?"

"Something like that," said Aaron. "There are dynamics in our society, things that are natural, innate. People born with certain power and status. The alphas are the top males. In each house, each pack, there's only one alpha per shifter type. The Beta males often challenge the Alpha, so there's always fighting among the groups. The alpha's job is to maintain order as well as to act as the Prime's generals. Omegas are the equivalent of an Alpha female. There are one or two per shifter group. They are more beautiful, more powerful, more fertile, and able to pass on better genes."

My head snapped up. For some reason, that caught my attention. "What?"

Aaron laughed and stood up. "That's what I thought. Always one way to get an alpha's attention." He turned away from me. "Of course, it's more than just the alphas and the omegas. There are betas too. Many betas are strong enough to challenge the alpha, and if one succeeds, it will become more powerful as its hormones adjust to its new rank. And deltas, too. These are the weakest shifters. They have weaker powers, are less insanely gorgeous, but compared to a human, they are still vastly powerful."

I nodded, finally able to get back onto my feet. My muscles were still trembling, and a strange sort of exhaustion swept through me. But it felt right, too. It felt like that is what I was always meant to do.

Aaron continued, "You'll learn more about them when you get to the Academy. That's what it's there for. It gives all kinds of history lessons. Tells you about the ranks, the houses, how to control your instincts."

"That anger," I said, with a burst of realization.

Aaron nodded. "And the lust."

"Lust?"

"It probably hasn't hit you yet," said Aaron. "But it will eventually. All alphas get it. This insatiable lust. Leftovers from when we had to claim and breed to survive. They'll teach you about it at Apex. Right now, my job is to just make sure that you know how to change, and you know how to defend yourself."

I remembered what he said yesterday. "From the people that culled my father."

Aaron nodded. "Exactly."

I tried asking, "Were you two close?"

But Aaron was uninterested in that, opting to instead launch into another explanation of how to handle myself. And that was the start of the hardest training in my life. I was rarely given a chance to look through the house after that first day, though the massive oil paintings clinging to the walls always managed to catch my eyes, and in the fleeting moments between getting up and eating, I could peek into this room and find a grand library, or peek into that room and find a study with ancient looking leather bound books. Dust motes drifted through the air no matter where I was at, and the whole house just seemed a little too empty, and a little too haunted.

But there was not much time for thinking or learning. It was like Aaron needed to keep me busy for a reason. Like he was trying to cram an entire lifetime's worth of training into the little time we had until classes at the Academy had started. And yes, I would be going. I had agreed to that already, and he had promised me that he would make sure all the papers were taken care of, and everything would be put together the way that it was meant to be.

Aaron had given me a smile when I told him that. It was the first time he had looked happy since I met him.

In fact, it was the only time that he had looked happy since I met him.

I guessed that between losing his wife and his brother, the guy was going through a lot. Any time I brought my father up, Aaron grew distant from me, and whatever conversation we had been having was shut down. I stopped asking after him, eventually. Things went a little more smoothly then.

Honestly, Aaron just didn't seem like the kind of guy who did a lot of talking.

He was okay when it came to explaining how to fight. And I could tell that he was really trying to explain the world of shifters to me, too. But outside of those lessons, he just didn't seem to have much to say.

The occasional bad joke, but that was it.

We were up early every morning and in late each day,

though we stopped at lunch to inhale a veritable banquet of meat. I got the impression that it was all stuff that he had caught himself, venison, bear, and hog.

There were mashed potatoes served with it, cooked in an old-fashioned manner. I got the distinct impression, when talking to Aaron, that he was an outlier. He stayed here alone, whereas most shifters lived in packs. He clung to this life with an iron grip, because it was the life that he shared with his wife, and he refused to move on, despite the fact that he could have. I wasn't sure if I admired him or felt sorry for him because of it.

That day at dinner, I tried something else. I asked him, "What was your wife like?"

"My wife?" Aaron asked, glancing up at me. He stabbed a piece of venison with his fork, hefting the whole cut up without slicing it into pieces. "Why?"

I shrugged. "I didn't get to meet her. I've only known my mom, far as family is concerned."

Aaron looked me over hard for a moment, like he was trying to figure out what I was really fishing for. Then he told me, "She was an angel."

It was hard not to laugh. I could hear the love in his voice. I asked her, "Did she do the cooking?"

"Every day. A big meal," said Aaron. "Didn't matter what was going on, she never served up anything less than this."

"And you don't either."

"Seems wrong to stop, just because she isn't around to do the cooking anymore."

"I'm sure she would have liked that."

Aaron laughed. "She would have hated my damn cooking. That woman only liked what she made herself. These potatoes would have all but done her in."

"That right?" I couldn't keep the grin off of my face.

Scooping up a spoonful of the potatoes, I told him, "They seem pretty decent to me."

"Only because you never got to have her cooking," said Aaron, happily. He smiled down at the plate. A misty look had entered his eyes. I could smell the sorrow on him.

Did you know emotions had scents? Neither did I, until about a week ago. Now I had started to take notice that everything around me had a scent to it. Even the way that people felt, if the emotion was strong enough.

Sorrow and grief. They had strong scents to them. It clung to Aaron no matter what we were doing.

Conversation died down after that. Neither of us really had anything to say to the other one. But it felt like an important conversation to have all the same.

Like we had finally managed to find some kind of... Common ground. A moment of actual kinship, instead of just saying that we were meant to be kin.

When we weren't eating, we were training.

Constantly. And I meant, **constantly**.

Six months wasn't a long time comparatively speaking, but when you were consistently putting in over a hundred hours a week into mastering new skills, anyone could make tremendous progress in that amount of time.

It wasn't just how to shift into my bear kin form and hold it, though that did take up a lot of my time and energy. Aaron also insisted that I needed to learn how to fight. Physically, with my hands and my feet. Aaron showed me everything from arm bars to how to throw a proper punch. He taught me how to use my knees and my elbows. And when those things were second nature, when I was able to start holding my bear form for longer, then he started to show me how to throw my weight around and use my bear form in a fight.

Each day, he had something new to teach me about how to handle myself. Aaron was a fighter. He had never been anything more than that. He was meant to hold himself to a higher standard. A general for my father, I thought, and a head alpha in one of the smaller clans that made up our greater pack. He was bear kin like me. It ran in the family, on my father's side.

I tried to ask what kind of shift my mother had been, but Aaron wouldn't answer. He made it clear that he didn't like talking about my mother. I wondered if she had been culled too, same as my father, or if something even worse had happened.

"You could give me something to go off of," I told him, late one day, as we were heading back to the house after a training session. "Tell me something about her that I didn't know."

"She isn't important," he told me. "You need to focus on your own training."

I snapped, "Was your wife unimportant?"

He froze. Came to a complete stop. A low growl bubbled up in the back of his throat. It was meant to be a warning, but I didn't back down.

"Don't ever say that my mom wasn't important," I told him, lowly. My growl echoed his. I should have backed down. He was bigger than me. Older. More experienced.

But I didn't.

That fire in my chest wouldn't let me.

Instead, I stared him straight in the eyes, and I told him, "You keep saying that I'm supposed to be the prime alpha and lead the House, but you won't tell me shit. How am I supposed to lead when I don't even know what's going on?"

"You aren't ready to learn about that," snarled Aaron.

The words came out half buried under a growl. He turned to face me, and his lips peeled back to show off his teeth.

Had they always been that sharp?

It was hard to tell.

Aaron continued, "I'm giving you more information than anyone else wanted me too."

"Who else?"

"That's not – stop asking so many fucking questions," Aaron said, unable to keep the frustration out of his voice. "I'm trying to get you to a point where no one's going to cull you the moment that you step off this property. What part of that is so fucking hard for you to get?"

"Try telling me who wants to cull me then," I challenged.

"Everyone!" snapped Aaron, finally losing his patience. He took a step towards me, grabbing me by the front of the shirt, and hauling me up against him. "You little shit. I know that this is going to your head. I fucking know it."

He exhaled hard through his nose, as though struggling with his own temper.

Aaron's voice dropped down into something that was low, but also sharp as steel. He told me, "The whole world is going to want you dead, the moment that they realize you're the prime. I have to get you ready for that. I can't waste my time telling you all this other shit, and you can't afford to spend your time thinking about it."

I countered, "I would think about it less, if I knew the truth."

Something dark flashed through my uncle's gaze. Whatever truth he was keeping from me, I could tell that it was weighing heavy on his shoulder.

"No." He dropped me finally, using his palm to straighten out my shirt in a petting motion, as though I was just one of his old hunting dogs. "No, you wouldn't. You would never stop thinking about it."

And then he turned and vanished into the house, leaving me on the path, even more confused and frustrated than I had been before.

Through all of our training, the fighting and sparring, the shifting and boxing, the necklace stayed around my throat. The triple eternity symbol felt like a message of some sort, though I had no idea what my mother would be trying to tell me. All I knew was that for the first time in my life, I had a piece of her with me.

It was one small change in a sea of many changes.

I was different. There was a change inside of my body. A physical reaction to the way that I was shifting. It felt like I had grown, like I had bulked out. Added height and muscle that clung eternally to my form. My hair became inky black, my skin turned a golden tanned hue, and when I looked in the mirror, I couldn't help but notice that my jaw had become more prominent, and my cheekbones had broadened.

There was something different about my mind, too. I had a new thought, a new urge, almost. I wanted to eat, but it wasn't just that. I wanted to hunt, too. I wanted to sink my teeth into something that had a beating heart. I wanted to be the one that ripped out its throat, that sent its blood splattering to the ground.

I threw myself into the training, destroying trees in my bear form and leaving my knuckles bruised when I was a human. I knew that my uncle had been telling the truth now. There was no denying something that was physically here, that was physically happening to me.

And that meant he was telling the truth about the other shit, too. About the Academy and about the house.

I wasn't able to get much information out of him regarding that kind of thing. Aaron didn't like to talk about politics. He didn't like to talk about lessons and history. He liked to fight, and that was about the extent of it. I couldn't fault him. I got the distinct impression that Aaron knew something bad was about to happen.

And... That made sense, didn't it?

I didn't know my father. Not really.

But he was Aaron's younger brother, and someone had killed him. In the middle of all this training, my uncle was mourning the loss of someone that he loved very much. And it was not the only loss he had felt, either. The pictures of Aaron's wife seemed to watch me whenever I was in the living room. I did my best to avoid them.

I thought that she was judging me for something.

Like whatever war was brewing, whatever fight was going to happen with House Blackstone, or had already happened, that was going to be on me.

Prime Alpha.

That's what Aaron seemed determined to call me. I was more than a normal alpha. I was stronger even than the senior alphas that taught at the school. I had a seed inside of my fire that would bloom into what our greater pack needed to not only survive but to thrive.

I just had to make sure that I made it to the Academy.

I had to make sure that I learned to control my fire, so it didn't burn me up instead.

6

Over the next few months, I found myself spending the majority of my time outside with my uncle, practicing my shifting. I was exhausted, but there was something about it that made me feel powerful, too. And more than that, it made me feel as though I was finally *whole*.

Something had been missing. Not my whole life, but the last year. I thought that it was just the pressures of college coming down on me, but now I realized that it was a lack of stimulation as I grew closer to being able to shift.

This morning was the first time that anything had changed since I arrived at Aaron's farm. The man was waiting for me down in the kitchen, same as he always was first thing in the morning. But he was wearing nicer clothes than I had ever seen him in; a pressed pinstripe button down shirt, and a heavy-looking canvas trench coat. His hair had been mostly tamed back, and he was making the same face that I did when I was frustrated over something, his upper lip curled back to show off his teeth and nose wrinkled just a little bit.

"What's going on?" I asked.

Aaron said, "I have to go deal with something in the city."

"Am I going with you?" I asked.

Aaron shook his head. "No. I'm settling a few things with an old friend of mine before you leave for the Academy. It shouldn't take long. I'll be back by the end of the day."

"An old friend. Someone that knows what happened to my father?"

"Yes."

"You're just determined not to tell me anything, aren't you?" I asked, frustrated.

Aaron told me, "I'm giving you the information that you *need* to know. The stuff that's going to keep you safe. Once I figure out if my friends are on board or not, I'll tell you about that, too. For now, just go through your shift work, and see what you can figure out without me holding your hand through it."

"You know," I said. "It wouldn't kill you to give me his name. I should know who my father trusted."

"You will, when you need to know about it," countered Aaron. "Right now, you don't."

"Says you," I grumbled.

Aaron snapped, "Damn right, says me. Says me, because I'm the one that's been living with these people since birth. Now it is not your fault that your mom went and took you elsewhere." He paused, licking at his teeth. Any mention of my mother put us both on edge. "But you have to get used to the fact that things are done differently here."

I told him, "That would be a lot easier to do, if you would actually tell me what *things* you're talking about!"

Aaron just shook his head. "I won't be back tonight, probably. If I am, it's not going to be until late."

In other words, the conversation was done. It didn't

matter what I thought about things. Aaron had already made up his mind. He wasn't going to tell me. And there wasn't anything that I could do to change that.

I was really getting pissed that Aaron wasn't telling me everything that was going on. I still didn't know who had culled my father, or anything like the location of the Academy. But I knew that when he decided not to do something, that was the end of it. The guy was seriously stubborn. The months spent with him had left me fully aware of the fact that he just wasn't going to tell me if he didn't want to tell me.

So, I waited for Aaron to leave, and then I headed out back. It was a nice morning out, at least. The sun was burning away the clouds that had been clinging to the sky the last few days. It looked like it wouldn't be raining after all.

I ran through my stretch routine first, trying to get myself warmed up. I rolled my shoulders, stretched my calves, and made sure to loosen my back too. Then I focused on changing into my bear kin form, letting the heat of the transformation rush over me. While there were partial shifts available, I was far more interested in the shift that allowed me to fully change into a massive bear-like creature.

It filled me with strength like nothing else ever had.

The change washed over me. It left me in the hulking form of something that *almost* looked like a bear. I was certain that an established hunter would have been able to tell that I wasn't truly a bear, but that wasn't my concern.

There was no one else around for miles, after all.

Something about taking on this form changed how I viewed the world. There was a whole new life waiting for me in these trees. The sensations washed over me. The colors were more vivid. The world seemed brighter, more alive. I could tell that there were birds in the trees, that there was a flock of sparrows flying on the other side of the thick branches.

It didn't take long for me to move away from the farm-house itself, and the old family property. I started out just taking my time. My goal right now was to learn how to hold the form for an extended amount of time.

Bear kins were strong shifters. We had a lot of physical endurance to offer the world. But according to my uncle, that makes it one of the most difficult forms to hold for any stretch of time, especially when you were first starting out.

So, each time I made that shift, I tried to hold it for longer than the time before. My running record at the moment was a two-hour block of time, but I had just been strolling through the woods for it. Aaron said that it would be more difficult to hold the form while I was in an actual fight.

He seemed to think that I would be doing a lot of fighting.

The Academy was going to teach me the majority of that. Aaron seemed to think it would be best to let the teachers handle everything complex. But I needed to know the basics, and I needed to have the stamina for those lessons.

After deciding that I had spent enough time just walking around, I broke into a lope. The ground was slightly disrupted by hillocks. They were thick with ferns. Loping over to one of them, I paused, tilting my head back and taking in the strong, impressive scents around me.

I lifted up my head, opening my mouth and breathing in through it. There was a scent on the wind, something that made my stomach growl. Aching with hunger, I left the property and went into the forest. The tangled trees don't have any paths leading through them, causing me to forge my own way. Something was thrilling about that. The way that the brush gave beneath my massive paws. The wind surged through my fur.

It felt like this meant something.

The scent grew stronger. I could place it now.

That was a deer!

For some reason, that filled me with joy like I had never known before. I changed direction, heading for the scent. And there it was – the deer! I could see it now!

The stag was a large, leggy thing. A massive rack of antlers was on its head. The fur looked soft. The meat was supple. My mouth was watering, drool running down the side of my mouth. I licked my sharp teeth and then moved for the deer.

I could hear the creature's heart beating in its chest. I could hear the birds on the wind. And I knew that this was what I had always wanted. Freedom in a way that I could never get when I was in my human form.

I threw myself forward, lunging. The deer's head snapped up, turning to look at me. It tried to run, but it was too late. Even the stag's long legs couldn't carry it away from me.

My massive body slammed into the side of the stag, knocking it down. I was on the creature in a moment, sinking my fangs into its neck. I was large enough that I could pick the deer up by the throat. I was powerful enough to shake it hard, sending blood spraying over the ground.

Copper rushed over my tongue. The deer blood was sweet. The allure of the meat was even better. The deer struggled for a moment, but with one more shake of my powerful head, its neck snapped.

I dropped the deer, looking over my kill. Blood seeped

from the wounds that my fangs had made. It dripped from my jaws, my fangs, and settled something inside of me that I hadn't even realized was unhappy.

Eating the deer seemed only natural. I hadn't just caught it to display my power. The shift left me constantly hungry. Starving, even. So, I ate the deer, and the meat was sweeter than anything else that I had ever tasted. It wasn't just fresh. It was mine.

I caught this deer. I had hunted it. It was my prey. My catch. My victory. I wanted to make sure that I ate all of it. When I had finished eating my deer, my maw was covered in blood. The fur on my muzzle and the front of my chest was damp with it.

Should I have done something with the bones?

I tilted my head to the side, uncertain what the right choice was. I didn't want to stay out there and bury it. After a few moments, I decided that the carcass would be best served left there. It would become food for the beetles that were moving through the dirt and the underbrush. The vultures, too. Things that could eat off of the remnants of my own catch.

I turned and started to make my way back towards the farmhouse.

After a few moments, I let my pace pick up. I went from a lope to a full out run. Branches snapped between my paws. I could hear better and see better in this form. My sense of smell was heightened to a ridiculous degree.

Each time I lurched forward, the muscles in my hindquarters bunched up and stretched back out. My claws churned up the earth as I ran, and the dried fallen leaves. Earth caked beneath my claws. My breath came in heavy puffs.

Stopping at the top of a slight incline, I looked around. My ears twitched, and I looked around.

This was my domain. This was my kingdom.

But it wasn't. The thought crept out of nowhere. I realized that this wasn't really my kingdom. If what my uncle said was true, then the Academy would be my true domain. He kept saying that I was some kind of a prime alpha.

That I was destined to be in charge. And in that moment, I could believe it.

The run back to the farmhouse was invigorating. My shift held the full way there. Maybe because I had eaten while I was in this form? Or maybe I was just getting stronger. It was hard to tell. Either way, I let my body drop back into that of a human man when I hit the backyard.

Strange tingles were running through my muscles. I rolled my neck a few times, popped my knuckles, and then headed into the house. That was the longest that I had ever held a shift, and the most I had done during one, too.

A quick check through the house proved that Aaron still wasn't home. His truck was gone. I couldn't scent him, either. For the first time since coming out here, I was able to take a rest in the middle of the day – a hot shower did wonders for my muscles.

Still no Aaron by the time I was done.

Dinner was leftover pulled pork that I fished out of the fridge, slathered in barbecue sauce, and served on slightly stale hamburger buns.

Still no Aaron.

Should I have been concerned? The fact that my father had been culled recently did make me slightly nervous about his absence. There wasn't anything to do but sit around and wait though. At least it gave me a chance to log into my favorite MMORPG for the first time in what felt like forever.

Touching base with my friends was something of a relief. Pendragon was even online! Laptop perched in my lap, I dropped onto the couch and pulled up our last PM exchange, fingers flying over the keyboard as I typed out a *hello* and invited him to join me on an excursion through the Crystal Caverns.

Thankfully, he accepted. And for a little while, at least, I didn't have to deal with shifters and missing family members.

7

It was almost midnight before Aaron pulled back onto the property. The twin lights from his high beams cut through the dirt on the front windows as he made his way up the long, winding driveway. The old vehicle was parked just in front of the porch. The hinges of the front door creaked as it was pushed open. My head snapped up like a dog that had just heard something interesting.

"You okay?" I asked. I was still sitting on the couch, with my laptop in front of me. Pendragon had gotten off a while ago, and I was just working through some of the smaller quests for a site-wide event that was going on.

Aaron grunted. Then, after hanging his trench coat up on the rack just inside the door, he nodded. "Went better than I was expecting."

"It must have been a long drive." I hit a few buttons to save my progress, shut off the game, and then closed my laptop. I sat it on the coffee table, next to the tall glass of lemonade that I had been sipping at.

"You kill something?" Aaron asked me, instead of answering. I wasn't sure if that meant it had been a short drive, and he had just been at his mystery friend's house for a while, or if it really was a long drive, and he thought that my statement was stupid.

"A deer," I said, unable to keep the pride from my voice. "A big old stag."

Aaron's nose wrinkles. "I can smell it on you. You're going to need to be better about that."

"I took a shower." The protest fell on deaf ears.

Aaron made his way over to one of the little end tables pressed to the wall. He pulled open the narrow drawer in front of it and grabbed a small glass bottle. It was roughly the size of his palm, a sphere with a top on it. The cork was glass, like the rest of the bottle. It didn't have a label.

"Young shifters like you don't think about it," Aaron explained. "But you're not a human anymore. Your senses are three times as high. More than that some-times, when you're fully shifted. That means other shifters are going to smell if you've fresh blood on you. And they could take it to mean that you're a threat they need to get rid of, or you're someone weak enough to get hurt."

"Right. But I *did* shower." I held up my hands, like that was going to prove my point. It should have. When I shifted back into a human, I had been soaked in sweat and the stag's blood. It had taken a good bit of effort to clear all of the red from my skin.

"You used my shit though. Scentless. The perfumes make me sneeze," said Aaron. He set the glass bottle down in front of me. "Use this after a hunt. Mild enough that it won't leave your senses clouded. Just enough to keep the blood off you."

"There's still a lot that I have to figure out, huh?" I took the bottle and rolled it between my fingers. It didn't have a label on it, but the stopper had a paw print stamped into it. Where did you even buy something like this?

"That's what the Academy is for. All I can teach you is how to fight. It's the academy that'll help you figure out your history. Help you figure out how to live in a pack or on your own. The shit like this, that you aren't going to know if you don't have an older shifter around." Aaron dropped down onto the couch next to me.

My mouth pulled into a thin line.

Aaron said, "I keep telling you, it's more important for you to focus on the things that you have to learn about the future, and not just the things that happened in the past."

"I could learn about both," I said, but the bottle was sat down on the table. I had to admit, I could see his point.

A little bit.

It didn't make all of the secrecy less irritating, but at least there might have been a reason for it. Hiding the smell of my hunt had never even crossed my mind. I figured that there were probably plenty of other things that had never crossed my mind.

A whole new world that I needed to figure out.

Of course, I wasn't about to just out and admit it. And I wasn't about to totally let Aaron get away without telling me anything.

I sniffed. "Who did you go see?"

"An old friend," said Aaron. "I told you that before I left."

"Right. And you said that you would tell me more about it when you got back."

Aaron groaned. But after a moment, he gave in. "Richmond Blue. He's a professor at the Academy."

I asked, "What does he teach?"

"Hand to hand. He's an asshole, but he knows what he's doing. And I've been friends with him since I was your age," explained Aaron. "You're going to need a few people there to look out for you. Make sure that no one outs you as prime before you're ready. He's one of the only people that are going to know you're the Prime."

"You trust him that much?"

"With my life."

"I mean, I guess you're trusting him with *my* life. Not yours."

Aaron laughed. "You have a point there. Alright, fine. Yes. I trust him with *your* life. He's a surly bastard, but he's not going to let anything happen to you. He'd make a good general for you, if he was about forty years younger."

A frown curled over my face. "You've mentioned those before. Generals."

"Mhm. Every prime has them. The alphas that you trust to help run your pack and keep things settled. You'll need to pick your own – and you'll need to be smart about it. Generals, they don't come around every day." Aaron explained. "It has to be someone that you would trust to die for you."

"People are really going to be trying that hard to kill me, huh?"

"Damn right they are. If someone kills the prime alpha, it gives them more fucking clout than anyone. And if the pack's unlucky, the next prime won't be ready to take over," said Aaron.

I asked, "Like I'm not?"

He shook his head. "Not like you. Like... a fucking five-year-old. Have to wait fifteen years before they start shifting. And in that time, you've got the asshole who killed the last prime running around, trying to make their house the most feared thing in the area. We got lucky, finding you so soon after your father... Part of why getting someone bred up young is so important."

The words caused something in my belly to twist up, a knot that was made of pure heat settling at the base of my spine. Though I couldn't see it, my pupils narrowed into mere pinpricks just at the mention of breeding someone.

Aaron either didn't notice my reaction or just didn't think anything of it.

He continued on, "You need to make sure that you've got a good heir, in case something happens. And the Academy, it will make sure that you know what you're doing. I need you to go."

"Okay," I said. The truth was, I'd made up my mind long ago that I would go. Saying it out loud seemed to settle something inside of Aaron, though. I could practically see the way that the tension eased out of his shoulders.

We each had a beer, then went to bed. Two days later, I found myself back in his truck and on the long road to the Academy. We didn't talk at first, not until after the second stop to stretch our legs and get something to drink.

Then, I asked him, "Who knows what I am?"

"A few of the teachers," said Aaron. "Blue, for one."

I nodded. "Right, but which others?"

Aaron shook his head. "Don't worry about it. You need to act like you don't know them, not like you've had someone fill you in behind the scenes. Leaving things a little secret, that's a good thing. Makes it easier for you to keep people from knowing that you're the prime. That's going to be the best way to do it. Just keep quiet about being the prime. I think we should get you through the first year without anyone else finding it."

Slurp. Sluuurrrrp. Sllluuuuurrrrp.

The last dredges of my red slushie were stuck in the corners of the cup. It burned at the back of my throat when I tried to suck it down.

"And what happens if they know?" I asked.

Aaron made a low sound in the back of his throat. It was almost like a growl. The words that followed were just as rough. "They're going to try and kill you, plain and simple. You can't trust everyone that you meet. And you're going to want to protect yourself, in every way that you can. Focus on your alchemy classes. They're going to be boring as shit this year, but it'll get better the longer that you're there."

"Alchemy? Like, turning lead into gold?" That had been briefly mentioned in the letter that Aaron had given me during our drive out to the family property six months ago. So much had happened between then and now, I had completely forgotten about it.

"Not quite. It's more of an ancient knowledge that allows alchemists and herbalists to create healing potions, poisons, and curses. Relics that get passed through the family."

"Do we have any of those relics?" I asked.

Aaron glanced at me. There was something strange about the look on his face. "I'm sure there are a few of them sitting around somewhere. Nothing that's important this year. You wouldn't know how to use them."

"That doesn't mean I shouldn't know about them."

"You'll know about them eventually," said Aaron, firmly. Before I could try and weasel any more information out of him, he added on, "That's not the only class you probably don't know about. It's more than just the hand-to-hand shit. Our world's complex. Got a whole class on artifacts."

"Like, mummies?" I asked. "Or are you talking about the Mona Lisa kind of thing?"

Aaron chuckled. "Neither. Mostly, artifacts include weapons but can also be things like portals, shields, armor, pendants. All can have various effects that can be used a single time or more powerful ones might be used again and again. Some create passive effects like increasing dexterity or movement. Gives you an added boost in a fight."

"And that's not the same as alchemy?"

"Nope."

"Okay." It was pretty obvious that I didn't know what was going on, but Aaron didn't seem inclined to answer.

He just kept going, "Then you've got the classes that teach you about gifts, and sorcery."

"Bullshit. Sorcery? Like, what, bibbidy bobbidy boo?"

"Take this shit seriously."

I snapped, "I am! But you're being vague about everything!"

Aaron made another sound in his throat and then shook his head. "Not on purpose. I'm used to talking to people who already know this shit. Sorcery. Not every shifter can do it. Some of us get a little bit extra when we're born. Some people think it's to try and get the alphas a bit closer to the prime, or to give deltas a chance to move up in the food chain."

"Okay. So, what kind of sorcery?" I asked. Honestly, all I could think about were the video games that I enjoyed playing.

"Some of them know how to heal," said Aaron. "All shifters heal rapidly of course, though some faster than others. Then you've got the precogs. Shifters with the ability to sense the future in visions, emotions, and dreams. Ability differs between people. I don't know much about that one. Others can communicate with animals or make plants do what they want. A few know how to draw upon the source of life in the world. The sorcery class, it shows you how to make use of that."

"I don't think that I have any of those."

"You're a prime, so you wouldn't. You'll still need to go.

Gives you a chance to look over the rest of your crew," said Aaron. "Let's you figure out who you want on your side, who's going to be a good pick for moving up in the ranks."

"Right. Are those... the only classes?"

"Fuck no. Got classes on history, that sort of shit. Arcane weaponry, hand to hand, SSD," explained Aaron. "Got a class on sparring, too, that one's important."

The lesson went on and on, through the remainder of the drive. I would ask him something about the Academy, and Aaron would flip a mental coin as to whether or not he was going to actually answer me. Sometimes, the answers were helpful. Sometimes, they weren't. But it was always something.

We had to stop and get a hotel on the way there, both of us in separate rooms. I was glad to drop backwards onto the mattress, even though it was lumpy, and it smelled more than a little bit like sweat. I was asleep before my head even fully settled onto the pillow.

And that night, I dreamed about running through the forest, about blood on my tongue, and about my mother. She was wearing the same necklace that I had taken from my uncle's house and worn since I found it.

She was trying to tell me something. I could see her mouth moving, but I couldn't make out the words. We were in a field. She reached out towards me, her mouth moving more frantically, like she was desperate for me to understand.

I reached out for her, but the field stretched out forever. I could hear wolves howling in the distance. A sword was thrust through her chest. And though I had not been able to hear her desperate pleas for me to do something, I certainly heard the way that she *screamed* as she died.

8

Apex Academy was hosted at a massive school, out in the forests beyond the main city of New York. It was beautiful as fuck, old stone and marble buildings, rich mahogany. The kind of place that you took one look at, and you knew was run from old money. Aaron didn't stay after dropping me off, just pointed me in the direction of the main staff building.

There was a man standing outside waiting for me. He was massive, almost seven foot and with the kind of broad shoulders that made it seem like he could knock someone down with a single flick of the finger. His hair was worn long and pulled into a bun at the base of his neck, starting to streak silver through the black of it. His eyes were a sharp, piercing blue. Massive claw scars ran over the curve of his face and down over the side of his neck. They vanished under his shirt, which was a nice enough looking white button down.

He had on a suit jacket over it, even though he was clearly not the kind of guy to pick that of his own free will. It must have been part of the uniform for teachers. He tilted his head back and sniffed the air, then held a hand out towards me. "Professor Richmond Blue."

"You're Uncle Aaron's friend." I said, taking his hand and giving it a firm shake. "I didn't think that I was going to meet you this soon."

"Someone had to come take care of welcoming you, and I wanted to take my measure of you," said Professor Blue. "See if Aaron was just jerking my chain or not. But he's right. You look just like both of your parents. Easy to see where you got the looks from."

I stood up a little straighter, finally taking my hand back when I was released. "Yeah," I told him. "From my mom."

It barely even got an upward twitch of the mouth. The guy was a hard nut to crack.

Oh well. It was worth a shot. And really, the joke was more for me than it had been for him.

After my mother passed away, I had taken solace in academic success, working my way toward law school.

Right then, law school seemed like a distant memory. I could only hope that the Academy here was at least *something* similar. Aaron had only given me the most basic run down on what the classes would be like, just enough to ensure that I didn't end up looking like a total dumb ass in front of everyone.

He led me through the double doors, and into the building itself. The main reception area was – well, stunning. That was the only way to describe it. Everything had this regal quality to it, straight down to the woman sitting on the other side of the desk.

She was tall and thin, with wolf ears that poked up through a mess of white hair. Her skin was thin with age, but there was something sharp about the look in her golden eyes. I wasn't sure if I would ever get used to that, the way that shifters looked once they had gotten control over their form.

"Professor Blue," said the woman. Her ears twitched with interest. She gave a sniff, and I realized that she was scenting the air to better try and figure out who I was.

"Agatha, this is our new student. Aaron's nephew," said Professor Blue. "Victor Rawlings."

She typed on the computer. A moment later, she nodded. "Yes, I just need you to sign these papers."

A stack of papers was passed over to me. The stack was thick, at least twenty or thirty of them, but they didn't all need a signature. A pen was handed over,

Agatha said, "By the time you finish, a student should arrive to show you to the dorms. You can ask them any other questions that you have."

"Thanks," I said.

Professor Blue gave my shoulder a reassuring clap. "It's all basic. I wouldn't worry about reading through any of it."

Agatha admitted, "He's right. You would have already consented to this in the opening package that we sent.

I didn't get one of those. I assumed that Aaron probably had gotten it and signed everything for me. At the end of the day, it didn't actually matter. The fact was, I wanted to be here. I wanted to know more about this world, about shifting, and about what Aaron had told me.

And I wanted to learn more about my family, too. I thought that I might be able to do all of those things if I just spent a little bit of time here.

By the time I sat down to start filling out the papers, Professor Blue had already left. It was mostly a lot of legal forms, standard paperwork, an NDA about who was attending and what rank they were. That kind of thing. I only skimmed through them, but they all seemed pretty basic and pretty legit. The last page mentioned something about *adhering to ancient claiming procedures* but that didn't make any sense to me either, so I just jotted down my initials and passed them back over to Agatha.

She was right.

I had barely traded the papers back over to her when someone else came in through the room. I smelled her before I saw her; a faint hint of peach, vanilla, and something sweet. The school here don't know that I'm the next Prime. House Blackstone has kept that secret.

Aaron, he had told me that there were other houses. Five of them, one for each brother. My house, it was the main pack for this country. There were other houses elsewhere, though, in different regions. Different primes there.

That means she just thinks I'm a regular alpha who has started here.

"Hey," she says. Her voice is sweet, but when I turn to look at her, I'm struck by the fact that she looks even sweeter. She's average height, large chest, long legs, and wide hips. Her silver hair has been left long and pulled into a braid on the side of her head. She has a strange marking on the back of her left hand, a wine-colored birth mark, and the tips of her painted nails look incredibly sharp.

She's wearing the female version of the Academy uniform. Her skirt is barely long enough to cover her ass, dark blue, with black knee highs that are ringed in silver. She has a suit jacket over the top of her silky looking blouse; the blouse is white, and the jacket is black. The braid is held in place with a dark blue ribbon, and her makeup is smoky but subtle.

She has small traces of fur here and there, though it is more like a velvet coating than rough fur. Silver ears poked through her hair, one on either side of her head. Her eyes might have been a stunning emerald green, but they were also slitted, like a cat's eyes.

When she smiled at me, it showed off a flash of sharp teeth. The insignia of the Academy is pinned to her breast lapel on the jacket; the same insignia that I remembered seeing in the email that they sent to me.

I was struck dumb by the sight.

She held out her hand. "I'm Petra Haliday."

"Victor," I told her, taking her hand. Her palm was soft and warm to the touch. "Rawlings."

Petra was gorgeous. And the way that she smells, it made something in my animal hind brain kick into being. "I'll show you where the dorms are at. Come on."

She led the way outside, and towards the east wing. The grounds were well maintained. There were other students milling around, bags over their shoulders. Most of them were walking around in groups, small clusters, talking with each other. They seemed to be sticking in groups of shifter phenotype, if their ears were anything to go off of.

The east wing was a large building with three floors, and a massive door at the front. At least half of the windows on the second and third floor had balconies attached to them. Some of the balcony doors had curtains drawn over them, the rooms clearly not in use.

As we walked, Petra explained, "I'm sure that they've already given you their usual spiel." She tilted her voice up, putting on a fake, posh accent. "Apex Academy teaches the other students how to become 'proper' alphas for their shifts; the goal is to ensure that the alphas will know how to handle themselves within shifter society."

I laughed. "Yeah, they did. How much of that is just pomp?"

"Well, that's mostly true. If you end up finding some-thing that doesn't fit-" Petra winked at me. "No, you didn't."

"So, turn a blind eye if people don't do what they're supposed to do." I asked, a little surprised by that.

"Right now, yeah. You don't want to catch anyone's atten-tion. You're a month late to the semester, but trust me... Something weird is going down." A strange look crossed her face when she said that, almost distant. "You'll be able to feel it in the air too, once you've been here for a while."

Feel it in the air?

Before I could ask her what she meant by that, Petra launched into the next part of the tour. She explained, "The alphas are given their own houses, the beta's have several dorms, and both the omegas and deltas live together in one larger 'block'."

"So, I get my own space is what you're saying." I said.

"The professor's figure it's that, or the whole school year is just always going to be a blood bath." She led the way into the east wing, then took me up onto the second floor. Our shoes thumped against the hardwood floor.

From there, Petra showed me to one of the rooms. She produced a key from her pocket and handed it to me.

The key was a heavy, ornate, brass thing. It was clearly very old and had the number four etched into it. The four was upside down, with a strike through it.

"That just means that you're a bear kin," she explained. "All of our shifts are numbered."

"What are you?"

"Lynx. That means I'm a three." She nodded at one of the other doors nearby, with a three on it. "That's a lynx's room, too."

"Yours?" I asked, a little excited that she would be so close to mine.

Petra laughed. "No, not mine. Just – someone's."

We only chatted for a few minutes longer, and then she left. I stepped into the room. It was larger than I had been expecting. There was a massive four poster bed, with an end table on either side of it. Heavy blue curtains hung over the windows, which were closed. It was as luxurious as the rest of the Academy.

This was clearly a place for people who were used to having money, big family homes, and power hooked to their last names.

My bag had been delivered to the room for me already; Aaron said that it would be. There were also several pairs of the Academy uniform sitting on top of the ancient looking dark wood dresser. I changed into one, pulling on the black slacks, the dark blue button up, and the heavy black jacket. I put the pin on my lapel, and then pulled on the dark gray socks and polished black shoes, too.

The uniform was pretty killer. I'd give the Academy that much.

There was a key card hanging on a hook. It stated that it would let me into the weapon's room, which was pretty fucking cool. The idea of getting a sword? That was incredible.

Like, who wouldn't want to get a sword? It seemed like it came straight out of one of my games. Obviously, they weren't going to just let me grab it and start swinging, but the thought was still exciting. A sword, that was my first idea, but I thought that I would be pretty alright learning how to use a bow and arrow, too.

It was a shame that I didn't have anyone here to ask about it. Like, whether they really let you just use them whenever you wanted, or if you had to follow a whole list of rules beforehand. Probably that, but hey, a guy could dream.

I would look pretty fucking killer walking around with a massive two-handed blade over my shoulder.

The bedroom had a large master style bathroom attached to it. The bathtub had jets built into it, and the towels were a dark red in color. It felt like every part of this room had been built for someone important. The fact that I was just some guy – just another alpha – in the mind of the staff and not the prime meant that this was just... Normal treatment. Everyone had a room like that.

A part of me felt a pang of grief. I didn't have a lot of good memories of my childhood, but I knew that my mother had been hard working, and had been always trying to make a better life. Before she got sick, she spent a lot of her time working. She was always at work, actually. I had a babysitter. And then the neighbor watched me. And then I watched myself.

She was always tired because of it.

She should have been able to do this. Not the Academy, clearly. But living somewhere like this, with such elegant furniture, and such an amazing bathroom. My fingers slid up, looping slightly around the necklace that I had on. I tugged the charm free from where it had been tucked into the front of my shirt, and ran the pad of my thumb over it.

My lips pursed together, and my eyes itched. I had to blink a few times.

"Come on, Vic," I told myself. "Stop doing this."

I had a whole new world to explore. I wasn't about to stand here and start crying, even though I happened to be thinking about my mom a lot. There was better shit for me to be doing.

I spent a little bit of time looking around, but I was way more interested in trying to get a look at the rest of the campus.

And, yeah, fine. I wanted to try and find Petra again, too.

She was *stunning*. And something about Petra, it had just clicked. Like she was meant to be part of me. It might not be that bad, if I got to spend more time around people like her! Every time that I thought about her, it made something in the back of my chest start to stir. I wasn't going to call it an instinct. It was more of an instinctive interest, or an absolute awareness of how much I happened to like her.

Plus, there was only so much poking around that could be done in this room. I figured that I would have a better time finding secrets out in the rest of campus. I tucked the necklace back under the front of my shirt, hiding the charm from sight. The golden strand around my neck was still visible, but that didn't bother me any.

I stepped out of the room and into the hallway. A few feet away from me, someone was leaning against one of the walls. He was tall but not broad, with the build of a runner. His silver hair was worn in a short crew cut, which made the ears that he sported seem that much more apparent. The stench of sweat and nicotine clung to him, but there was something almost fruity beneath that, the barest hint of apples and oak leaves. He was wearing the same uniform as me, though he didn't have his jacket on.

"There you are," said the guy. "I guess they were right. We do have a new bear kin in the house."

"Guess so. The name's Victor. And you're?" I tilted my head to the side, trying to size the guy up. It felt different, meeting someone here as opposed to meeting someone at my law school. Back there, we were all struggling to figure out the heavy leather bound textbooks that were being thrown at us. Here, it felt like being in a competition with the rest of the world long before you even actually got to meet them.

"Jakarta," he answered. "Jak."

"Jak, huh?" I made a note to not forget the name. He didn't smell like a bear. He had the same faint tinge to him as Petra. So, I figured that he was probably a lynx shifter. "Did you come up here for a reason, or what?"

"Already told you. I just wanted to see if the rumors were right,' said Jak. He took a step towards me, making no small show of looking me up and down. I had to fight the urge to bristle beneath his gaze.

I wasn't going to start a fight. Not like I did back at that party. Certainly not on my first day at Apex Academy, and before this guy even *did* anything.

Not liking how someone looked at me wasn't enough to break their nose. Even though a part of me really, really wanted to do that. Maybe *that* was just the instinct of an alpha. Or a prime alpha, I supposed. Being able to assert dominance like that, it must have been a big deal.

Jak finally finished looking me up and down. It was hard to tell if he liked what he saw or not. He said, "People are already talking about you."

I frowned a little bit. "Is a new student that big of a deal?"

"You're getting here way later than anyone else," said Jak. One shoulder bunched up into a shrug. "And your name has some pretty heavy connections to it. Rawlings, huh?"

He fished a lighter out of his back pocket. It had a metal casing around it, which was designed to look like a snake. The mouth opened up over the top of the lighter, looking as though it was spitting fire every time he clicked it.

"Yeah, Rawlings." I didn't like this guy. He had a bad vibe to him. The kind of instinctual distaste that I was learning not to doubt. It turned out that I had a way better sense of people now than I ever did in the past.

All it took was a sniff of them and a glance in their eyes.

Click, went his lighter. My chest got tight.

Click, it went again. I wanted to reach out and take it from him.

Jak gestured towards the stairs. "You and I should talk. I'll show you where the dining hall is on the way."

If I wasn't so hungry, I would have told him no on principle, because his vibes were really THAT bad. Like something about him, it just rubbed me the wrong way. Maybe it was the way he smelled. Maybe it was the look on his face.

I wasn't sure, exactly.

But I was starving, and a part of me wanted to know more about this guy. Exactly why his vibes were so bad.

So, I agreed to go with him – and Jak flashed me a smug looking smile before he turned and led the way back down the stairs, and to another section of the Academy's main building entirely.

9

The dining hall was a large room, with two long tables in it on either side, like an old-fashioned cafeteria, and then a slew of smaller tables scattered around the outskirts of the room. The smaller tables were square and each had only two chairs at them. Mated couples sat at these tables – and couples that were flirting so hard, they were clearly *trying* to make it a little bit further.

Like the rest of the Academy so far, the dining hall appeared to be opulent and rich. The walls were of dark wood, and the floors were marble. There was an eatery at the far end of it. A portly man was on the back side of the counter, looking rather bored. His thinning, wiry hair was pushed out of his face, and he had a hand propped up against his chin. His other hand was idly trying to fill in the spaces on a word puzzle.

As we approached, he asked, "What's a three-letter word for a female farm animal? Ain't hen or cow. I tried those already."

"Ewe," I suggested. "Or sow."

The man looked up. He had a blind, misty blue eye.

There was a bit of scruff under his chin. Dark red scales were visible on the sides of his neck, and his cheek. The man was a saurian shifter. "Ewe, huh? Hadn't thought about that one."

He scratched the word into the proper boxes.

Jak said, "How about something to eat?"

"You're late," said the man, without hesitation. "You know what time we serve up."

I raised a hand. "That's my fault. I just got here."

"No shit?" The man asked.

I nodded.

Jak said, "Come on, Haverty. Have a heart. Get us a plate of something. I've spent all day showing this guy around."

That was a flat out lie. Petra had shown me around.

Not wanting to start trouble right away though, I bit my tongue.

The man, Haverty, gave a heavy sigh. He put the pen down and stood up. Ignoring Jak, he turned to me and said, "We serve breakfast at eight, lunch at noon, and dinner at six. You want to eat something outside of those times, you're going to have to make it yourself. You've got a little kitchen in your room, and you can place an order for food."

There was a large clock on the wall in the center, between the two tables. It was three in the afternoon. "I can wait until six."

Haverty seemed surprised by that.

Probably because Jak instantly started to protest. "Come on, there's no way that we're going to wait until six, when it's not our fault that we missed lunch."

Haverty's lips pursed together. His good eye, reptillian in make, slid to the side and stared hard at Jak. Then back at me. "You can wait?"

I was starving, but the last thing that I wanted to do was

start having issues with people before my first day of classes even officially started. So, I told him, "Yeah, I can wait."

Haverty pointedly sat back down.

Jak groaned, but had no choice save stepping away from the front counter. "We should have just insisted. The guy works for the Academy. That means he works for us."

"I think it means that he works for the dean, actually," I said, with a huff of laughter. "I don't think anyone on staff works for the students."

Jak shook his head. "No way. We're the ones that fund this place. Our money keeps everyone here employed. That means we pay their checks, and they work for us."

Yeah, I fucking hated people with that mindset. They were not only pricks – they were the kind of pricks that liked to throw their weight around.

Not wanting to get into it, I gave a noncommittal shrug. "Where *were* you at lunch time? Because it wasn't actually with me."

Jak shrugged. "I was doing some extra credit work for one of the teachers. So it technically still wasn't my fault that I missed it. They kept me longer than they should have."

He looked across the room, and nodded at a few other guys. They smelled like lynxes, too. "I'm heading that way. You should come with me. I'll introduce you to some of the cooler guys on campus."

"I'll pass," I told him. "There was a vending machine out on the side of the building. I'm going to go snag something from it and try to figure out where to order food for my room at."

Jak pursed his lips together, clearly unhappy with that decision – but then he turned and made his way over to his friends. They greeted Jak warmly.

I didn't have anything against meeting my fellow

students, but I absolutely had no interest in meeting the kind of guys that thought Jak was cool – or vice versa. In my opinion, he was obviously a low life, the kind of guy that you wanted to avoid however you could, whenever you could.

I made my way back outside, stepping around to the side of the dining hall and seeking out the metal box that I had seen gleaming in the distance earlier. I stepped over to it, perusing the wares.

Cans of soda. Bags of chips. Packages of cookies. It was the usual affair for a vending machine on a college campus. A few of the bars were clearly marked gluten-free, which I thought was pretty amusing considering the fact that we could just go and *catch* food out in the forest.

And yeah, I'll admit. It crossed my mind that I could just change into my bear kin form and go out into the woods to hunt something. I could tell that there were deer in the trees, and other forest wildlife. But... I knew that sticking around on campus for the first day was the best thing to do, especially as I hadn't been given the all clear by any of the people in charge that I could leave.

There was just one problem.

Once I picked out what I was going to get – a lemon lime soda, and a bag of cheese crackers – I was faced with the fact that it didn't take money. There was, instead, a slot for a key.

"Fuck." I poked at the key for a moment. "Are these not for the students?"

"It runs on your room key," said a familiar voice.

"Petra!" I gave her a smile when I turned around, excited to see her again.

Petra gave me a bashful smile of her own. "I figured that there was probably a lot about the Academy grounds you didn't know yet, and when I saw you over here, well-" She shrugged. "I had to ask Haverty about it. I thought that you needed a special key from him to use it."

I fished the room key out of my packet and stuck it into the machine. When I turned it, the machine whirred to life, and my can of soda and package of crackers toppled off of their shelves and were unceremoniously tipped out of the machine and into the pick-up bay.

"Sweet." I shoved the key back into my pocket and then got my drink and my crackers. The can hissed when I cracked it open. "How do they keep track of it?"

Petra shrugged. "You get thirty uses a month. When you run out of uses, it just stops working. I don't know if the keys themselves are that individual to the machine, or if it's charmed or what but – what's the look for?"

"Charmed, huh?" I asked. "And here I thought that part of things was just a bullshit story my uncle was telling me.

Petra laughed. "You can turn into a bear, but magic is where you've decided to draw the line?"

"I mean – I haven't *seen* any magic yet," I countered.

Petra shook her head. "You've seen it. You just haven't recognized it. Come on."

She turned and started to walk down the path, towards the front and main section of the courtyard. I followed after her, popping open the crackers, too.

Petra snagged one of them. "You remember those signs that you saw on the way in?"

I nodded.

"They're wards. Look here." She stopped and pointed at several of the stones in the path that we were walking on. They bore the same symbols that had been on the signs my uncle and I passed earlier. One of them was a star with three vertical lines through it. Another one was a line-drawn tree, simple, no leaves, and a sun burst behind it. And the third one resembled a three that had been turned upside down, with two vertical lines balanced above it; none of the lines were touching.

Petra pointed to the star with three vertical lines through it. "This one is hooked to something in the dean's office, and it rings any time someone comes up the drive."

"Like magical bottles on a rope," I joked. In hindsight, I was pretty certain that my uncle had a few of those stars carved into the trees on his property.

"Right." Petra pointed to the line-drawn tree with the sun burst behind it. "This one helps cloak the Academy, so people pull up and don't understand what they're faced with. I don't really know if they're tricked into thinking that the Academy is meant to be here, or if they think that they've gone to the wrong spot, or what. It's a complicated one."

"I don't like the idea of something that can mess with a person's memories," I said. "Or their understanding of the world."

"I don't either," admitted Petra. "But it's better than having hunters show up here at all hours of the night, and then not being able to explain what this weird Academy is doing out here in the woods. I mean, can you imagine what would happen if they saw one of the lycans? We would end up on the next *Weird Wonders* for sure."

A grin spread across my face. "I like that show."

Petra's eyes went bright. "Do you really?" With a nod from me, she said, "I thought that the season was killer. The episode about the Jersey Devil was terrifying."

"I liked the one with the wendigo," I said. My favorite episode was actually about the dissection of myths in which dragons kidnapped hapless maidens and brought them back home, but it was a pretty controversial piece so I left it out of the equation.

Petra and I became so engrossed in our conversation about *Weird Wonders* that we completely forgot about the original discussion. Before we knew it, the both of us were rushing back into the dining hall, and then up to the counter.

This time, Haverty was already up and standing. He slid a laminated menu towards us. "Make it quick. I've got a lot of mouths to feed."

"The venison burger," I told him, without even thinking about it. I had developed a real taste for deer while staying with my uncle.

"You're going to regret that before long," said Petra. She ordered the pizza, heavy on the sauce.

Haverty vanished into the back. I assumed that he must have kept the food frozen and just had to heat it. That didn't bother me. I was used to the kind of food that was served at colleges.

"Why?" I asked. "I like the deer."

Petra explained, "Because it's all that you can hunt out here. And the stronger a connection you make with your shifted form, the more those instincts are going to become part of you, no matter what life you're holding onto. That means you're going to find yourself wanting to hunt the deer all the time – and desperate for something else later."

"It sounds like I have a lot that I need to figure out still," I told her, with a shake of the head.

Petra smiled and promised, "Don't worry. I'll help you."

10

Petra quickly became one of my best friends at the Academy. We had classes five days a week, three classes each day. There was plenty of time between the classes to train on your own, and different buildings for the different ranks of shifter to sleep in. And she was pretty good about answering most of the questions that I had.

Granted, Petra was a student too – but she came from a long line of shifters. Her family hadn't tried to keep her ability a secret, either, which meant that her parents had already answered the base questions about instincts that I had.

She was also keen on showing me around, teaching me all of the different things that were tucked away on campus.

A shortcut between the Alchemy building and the dining hall. A secret hollow in the library that couldn't be seen from anywhere, no matter how hard you looked. A glade in the forest surrounding the campus that was prone to a family of deer showing up, meaning it was prime hunting grounds.

"I don't know," said Petra, one day, after I asked her if she thought that the Academy was holding up to its big, fancy title. The place was pretty massive and the classes were amazing – learning to use the items in the weapon's room was like something out of a dream.

Still, the letters had hyped it up a lot. I hadn't yet decided whether it was *really* worth all that fuss. It sounded like Petra hadn't been able to figure it out yet, either.

I laughed. "You don't know?"

"I've only been here two months," admitted Petra. She never lied to me, or tried to hide what she was feeling. I liked that about her. There was no guess work involved with Petra. "And I can see why it's the best place for shifters to learn. It just still seems lonely sometimes."

"Yeah, I know what you mean. Do you miss home?"

"I do." The corners of her mouth twisted up into the prettiest smile that I had ever seen. "I have a younger sister at home. She's going to come here too, once she's old enough."

"Is she still in high school?" I asked, curious. We hadn't talked about family very much. I didn't like to talk about mine, so I never thought to talk about others.

"No, she's not that much younger. Thankfully," laughed Petra. "I'm not great with little kids. I wouldn't know what to do with her." A pause, and then, "She's only a year younger than I am, but she had a late bloom with her shift. She's not going to start attending the Academy until next year at least, maybe the year after that."

"A late bloom?" I hadn't heard that term before. Not that I was surprised. I was still learning a *lot* of the different terms that the shifting society used.

"Most people develop their shift when they hit a milestone age," explained Petra. "Sixteen, eighteen, and twenty-one are the most common. Anything after twenty-one is considered a late bloom."

"So, that's what I would be," I said, with a nod. We were walking towards our first class of the day. Early morning sunlight was still casting its glow on the grounds around us. There were songbirds in the trees and dew on the grass.

The mornings seemed different, now that my senses had awakened on a new level. It was all more clear, and more alive.

Petra nodded. Her ears twitched. "That's right. You would be a late bloom."

"Damn, they should have – I don't know. A dictionary with all of this stuff in it." I told her, with a laugh.

"I mean, the parents normally teach their kids," said Petra. There was a question in her voice. She wanted to know why my father hadn't taught me anything about it.

I had already discussed the story with my uncle before coming here. The lie came smooth, "my mother ran off when she was still pregnant with me. I never met my father."

"Oh. Your mother didn't tell you about it?" Petra asked.

I shook my head. "No, but she died when I was young. I think maybe... she thought that I wasn't going to ever shift. Late bloom and all that."

"Duds," said Petra, with a nod. "Every shifter's parent worst nightmare."

I asked, "Is it really that big of a deal to have a kid that can't shift?"

"I mean, not like... Not like *really*?" Petra made a face. "It's not like it brings shame to the family or anything? But we have a violent lifestyle. Fighting is common, especially with alphas. So, if your kid can't defend itself against a shifter, things get more complicated."

"I guess that makes sense," I told her. "Seems like it would be easier to follow laws about not hurting kids, especially if they can't shift."

Petra's shoulders jerked in a shrug. "Think about the laws we do have right now, and how many people don't follow them. There's nothing to say that they would listen to other more specific laws."

One of the reasons why I liked Petra so much was because she always seemed willing to discuss the world with me. She didn't mind theorizing what could happen if something changed, or helping me figure out exactly why things happened a certain way.

After that conversation, she was even more willing – now that she knew I hadn't been raised in the world of shifters.

And soon enough, life fell into a pattern. The Academy was almost painfully routine.

We had classes in the morning, and electives in the afternoon. Breakfast, lunch, and dinner were held at set times in the dining hall, though you could go into the woods and hunt your own prey if you needed the extra protein. I caught Petra coming back from it once, still in her animal form.

She had been gorgeous. Like, the kind of stunning that stole the breath straight from your lungs. She was large, six feet, maybe a little more than that, with silver fur that was riddled through with black. The maroon wine birthmark on her hand showed up in her shift form, as a large blot of almost purple fur on her left paw, in the same shape.

Even if she didn't have that though, I would have known that it was her. Petra smelled more like peach pie than anyone else that I had ever been around. It always made my mouth water.

A part of me couldn't help but think about what Aaron said about breeding and claiming and getting myself an heir soon as I could. Maybe it wasn't just the smell of her that was making my mouth water. It was all of her.

It was the *thought* of having all of her.

There was only one real problem: I wasn't the only one that had noticed Petra.

It wasn't a surprise. It just seriously irritated me. Every time I went out to try and find Petra, it seemed like Jak had already done that. And he was gross about it, always trying to put his hands on her shoulders and getting up in Petra's personal space. At one point, I heard him talking about how much his family valued traditions.

I didn't know entirely what he was talking about, but the phrase had Petra growling at him and making a hasty retreat. Her lack of interest didn't dissuade Jak.

That was a problem for me.

I was still figuring out how this world worked. I understood that the whole concept of mating was highly valued within shifter society, but I also know you weren't supposed to treat women like that. It drove me mad, the way Jak was always leering at her.

Late one Thursday, I was coming out of one of the elective courses that Aaron had signed me up for. It was on the history of enchanted items, which I guess he figured a prime alpha should know about. I was silently lamenting how boring I found the topic when I caught a whiff of Petra. She smelled just as sweet as ever – but the scent of Jak right next to it made a low growl build in my chest.

After taking a moment to swallow down the sound, I went in search of them.

I found Petra standing against one of the walls in a great arched indoor hallway. She had her shoulders pressed to the wall behind her, and her tufted lynx ears flat against her head. Her eyes were narrowed.

Jak was standing in front of her, one hand on the wall by her shoulder, leaning into her personal space. He was purring, but there was something ugly about the sound. Like a can of rocks being rattled together, instead of the usual comforting allure that a cat's purr might bring.

"Come on, honey," said Jak, in a low, sour honey tone. "Don't be like that. I could give you the best time of your life."

The thing about an Academy like this was one was that you got to know everyone pretty quickly. Or at least, you got to know about them through word of mouth. Three months into the semester, it had been pretty much decided that Jak was the kind of guy I didn't want anything to do with.

Some of the other shifters said that he was 'old school', which was just a nice way of saying he was an absolute asshole.

"I don't want to breed with you, creep," Petra spat. The words were sharp and acidic, but they didn't seem to deter Jak at all. If anything, he seemed more interested in her once she got all fired up. Maybe it was fun for him. I didn't know. It was hard for me to get into the head of someone like that.

He told her, "You're only saying that because you haven't seen how skilled I am under the sheets. You and I could be great together, Petra. My family loves yours. Our kin have always been eager to join with each other."

"I'm *not* my aunt," insisted Petra. She could probably overpower him if she shifted, but Petra had already mentioned that she wasn't much of a fan when it came to fighting and violence in general. She was a runner, a hunter, and – though she didn't want most people to know – a bookworm. "And I don't want to do this with you, Jak. Take a hint and fuck off."

I reached out, placing my hand on his shoulder. With a single firm yank, I was tugging him a step away from Petra. She let out an audible sigh of relief to not have him in her personal space any longer.

Jak spun around snarling. Before he even took stock of the situation, he shoved me in the chest, hard. "Fuck off, bear kin! No one asked for your input here!"

"I think you should start listening to what she tells you," I said, frowning. A low growl rumbled in my own throat. It was hard. My first instinct was to throw myself forward and slam into the guy, maybe even skip the fighting and just try to outright rip out his throat.

That wasn't going to actually get me anywhere, though. I exhaled hard through my nose, trying to swallow the snarl back down.

"Mind your own business," Jak snapped. "I'm talking to the *pussy*cat, not to you."

Petra hissed at him.

Jak was still standing in front of her. She wouldn't be able to easily leave.

Our gaze met.

I didn't want to just come out and fight this guy. I didn't think that Petra wanted that, either.

She seemed to get her nerve back a little bit, slinking around Jak. He frowned after her, but let her go past him.

Petra told him, "You want to get a mate, you need to work on your manners. I don't know what your uncle has been telling you, but this isn't the forties anymore. No girl wants to be picked up just to pop out a litter for you."

Jak seemed to fumble at that. Something about his scent

changed, as though he had become unsettled. "What do you know about my uncle?"

"I know he's a real piece of work," said Petra. "And that my Aunt might have wanted to stay at home and be a perpetual mom, but that's *not* what I'm looking for. Go find someone else to be your *little pussycat*."

She said the last two words with so much distaste in her voice, it was almost a physical thing dripping off of her tongue.

I didn't think that it was Petra's dismissal that had him so rankled. It was whatever she had brought up about his uncle. That was weird. I wondered who his uncle was? I didn't have a lot of time to think it over before Petra turned and vanished down the hallway.

I didn't wait around to deal with Jak, turning and heading the other way. A part of me wanted to go after Petra and make sure that she was okay, but I was worried that it might make her feel stifled, or maybe like I was trying to pull the same shit as Jak. And that was so not the fucking case.

Stepping outside, I realized that a storm was going to be blowing in soon. Thick black clouds were building in the sky above me. They hadn't totally blocked the sun out yet, but it was definitely going to happen. The astronomy students were going to have to miss their class, if they didn't clear up fast.

My maw parted, almost instinctively. I could taste the rain on the back of my tongue. I could smell the way that the storm was going to be brimming with electricity. It would be a lightning filled mess, that was for sure.

Not wanting to get caught out in this weather on a hunt, I decided to head to the library instead. It was located in the west of the Academy grounds. The inside was massive, with three floors that were filled up with bookshelves. Some of them were ancient tomes, with cracked leather on the bindings and faded engraved titles. Others were newer, freshly laminated pieces.

The very top floor had the oldest books on it. The middle floor had several rows of computers that could be used with the librarian's approval. And the bottom floor had a study area, which was filled up with plush looking red armchairs, and several lounges as well.

A week in, and I was still trying to figure out everyone's name. Knowing the other shifters was of great importance. I figured that if I was going to be their prime alpha at some point, I had better get to know them better, right? Figure out who was who, what they did, what they *could* do later on. That kind of thing.

The library was actually a pretty good space for that to happen. The thing about it was that people came up here, they did their own thing, and they left. That made it easy for me to watch them from my own desk. Their scents were always unique. I had figured out how to tell what sort of a shifter someone was by their scent alone.

Once I figured out what their shift was, it would be easy to ask around the next day and get a name for them, too.

One of the chairs was occupied by a lycan shifter named Bree. She had a great ass on her, and the kind of curves that are just *wow*.

Her blue hair was almost mane like in appearance, thick, a bush of it that was just unkempt enough to be sexy. A very eighties bed head kind of vibe. Her ears were massive and furry, and her tail was a thick bush of a thing, sticking out from the bottom of her skirt. The bulk of her tail caused her skirt to hike up a little too high, showing off a flash of her panties. She was in here a lot when I came by, though I didn't think it actually had anything to do with schoolwork. I thought it was more for some kind of personal thing.

Even bookworms didn't spend that much time studying – especially not when over half of our Academy classes were physical in nature, teaching us how to hunt and fight and wield weapons of every sort. Definitely a personal project.

I stepped past her, heading to the second floor. I hadn't been on the computer since showing up, and it felt like a raid might be the perfect way to unwind from all of this. Every time I blinked; I could see Jak up in Petra's personal space. I could hear the way that she wanted him to leave.

My fingers flew over the keyboard. I swiped my Library Pass and logged in using my personal student code. Before long, I was signing into my account on Azenar. It didn't look like Pendragon was on, but I had a couple of messages from my usual raiding buddies. They were trying to figure out why I had suddenly gone AWOL. They didn't understand. I had never just STOPPED getting on before.

Considering I was one of the top players on the whole site, my sudden absence hadn't gone unnoticed. It had left a dent on my scores too, dropping my listing down by a whole two points. A single raid wasn't going to be enough to bring me back up in the slots. I was going to have to try and get on here more often.

Otherwise, all of the hard work that I had put into things over the years would be for nothing. My class would stay the same and so would my level, but I would end up losing my place on the National Azenar Ranking Board – and really, that's where the majority of my clout actually came from.

One of the messages that had been sent to me had even mentioned as much, pointing out I was sliding down the numbers and asking if everything was good with me.

After organizing the raid and responding to the

messages, it was actually pretty easy to lose myself in the game. Azenar had always been my escape – after my mother died, after the car crash, any time it felt like something was missing or wrong. When I just needed to get out of my own head for a while.

It was easy to fall back into the routine.

At least, it had always been easy before. Now though, I couldn't help but wonder if a run through the woods would do a better job at helping me sort out my thoughts. The loud rumble of thunder outside was the only thing that kept me from checking, and the only reason that I stayed on Azenar late – late into the night.

It was something that I would come to regret the next morning. I knew that much. While a lot of our lessons were about shifting and fighting, the more academic based classes still gave out traditional homework. Topics to research. Essays to write. Tests that had to be passed.

You couldn't actually fail the Academy, not like a traditional university, but the Dean wouldn't let you leave with the credentials needed to start your own pack if you were an alpha with a low score – and if you were an omega or a delta that didn't pass, the chances that anyone would want you in *their* pack was pretty much next to nothing.

Not to mention the fact that families held each other to high standards. Honor was a big deal for shifters. You didn't want to be the first alpha in your lineage that didn't pass at the end of your first cycle through the Academy. Your kin would never let you live it down.

So, was there something that I should have been doing other than playing my game? Without a doubt.

As a late bloom, I had to do twice the amount of studying that a normal shifter my age would require. But at that moment, I just couldn't make myself do it. Sometimes, playing my game was the only thing that kept me rooted to my old life.

I liked the people that I knew in Azenar. I liked the familiarity of it, too.

So, I would skip studying tonight, and I would skip sleeping at a decent time. Just for a little while, I would have something that felt more normal.

11

The world still smelled of petrichor. The storm lasted most of the weekend, only clearing up late on Sunday night. Monday morning came with thick puddles and stretches of mud on the ground. That didn't stop me from being hyped about the day's lesson plan. It's held outside, and it's the first Hand-to-Hand class we've had that's going to cover our shift forms, and how to maintain them under duress.

Professor Blue had all the students gather around him. I was paired up with a lynx shifter named Davis Thompson. He was tall and lean like most of the lynx shifters were, but he was only a beta. His short silver hair was almost always gelled up into spikes, though the crust was gone by the time that he'd shifted once.

Our training was simple. We shifted and did laps out in the forest. It was obvious to everyone that I had a natural talent for my shift. That I could hold myself to a higher standard than the others. The time that I had spent training with my uncle had clearly paid off. At least those six months hadn't been for nothing.

Still, it didn't stop me from feeling starved when I

changed back into a human. I got back about three minutes before Davis did. His shift fell apart almost as soon as he made it back. I grabbed and helped steady him while he caught his breath, and then he waved me off.

"I'm good." Davis waved me off. We were dismissed from Professor Blue's class once everyone made it back and sent off towards one of our history lessons instead. I had barely left the training field before Davis came rushing up to me.

I flashed him a grin. "You good?"

"I'm good," said Davis. "Just still figuring that shit out."

"You're getting faster though. And you beat out a bunch of the other lynx shifters," I said.

Davis nodded. "Yeah, but I didn't get ahead of Jak."

The mention of Jak made something sour curl in the back of my chest. I had to swallow back the growl, before it could affect our conversation. It wasn't the first time that I had chatted with Davis before. I liked the guy.

Not enough to sit next to him once we got to class, though. I sat next to a woman named Cass.

Cassandra White was a bear kin like me, and only an inch shorter, too. Her red brown hair was perpetually worn up in a bun, and she was muscular enough that the sleeves of her jacket looked like they were borderline too tight. We hadn't spoken to each other yet, but I had taken note of the way that she smelled like the pecans she was always eating, and something sharper, almost like blood.

She was my go-to history class buddy. I knew that if I was sitting next to her, I would be able to actually focus on what was going on up at the front of the classroom. If I sat too close to Jak, that sour feeling in my chest took over, and I found myself glaring at his back the whole lesson.

And I figured that she must have liked sitting next to me

in class too, because she always kept the seat at her side empty for me.

The teacher was a saurian shifter named Eric Balboa. He was short and broad, stocky, with red hair and small scales in the same color near his ears, slitted eyes, and a long tail that curled out from a slit cut into the back of his trousers. He had no fangs but a strong jaw.

He clapped three times, signaling that class was starting.

"Everyone, be quiet," said Professor Balboa. "I don't want to hear a peep, growl, or sniff out of you unless you're asking a question. Today's lesson is important. We're going to be discussing the variations of shifters, and common traits. The purpose of this lecture is to help you untangle some of the things that you have likely been feeling since your first shift."

Some of the other students weren't interested. They were the ones that had been raised by other shifters. At least half of the students were like me though and didn't understand how the shifter society worked. These lectures were a little hard to get through, but they were super important, and they would continue to be super important as time passed on.

Professor Balboa explained, "The primary shifter forms are bear kin, lycan, saurian – like myself, lynx, and avian. All types can shift, turning them into a full were-beast. That means being able to both stand and fight upright as well as run on all fours. I know that the movies might have led you to believe that this is a bad thing, or perhaps looks different than it actually is. With any luck, you'll have figured out by now that is far from the truth."

He was right. This isn't anything like movies that show off various werewolves. I often thought about an old horror movie called *Ginger Snaps* when I thought of the lycans –

but the girl in the library was nothing like the werewolves in that film.

Professor Balboa continued, "Many of you will have noticed that your physical appearance in your human form has changed now that you have undergone your first shift. This is because our human forms reflect shifted forms. An example would be my hair." He ran his fingers through the bright red locks. "Which is not dyed, but changed to this color when I was your age and underwent my first shift."

Yeah. My hair turned black after my first shift. I got bigger, too. Taller, stronger. A different set to my jaw. A different set to my eyes. It was strange, but it was kind of nice to know that it wasn't just a me thing. Everyone had to deal with this.

It was like – what, shifter puberty?

Weird, but easy enough to remember and understand.

"That is not the only thing you will notice now that you have shifted," said Professor Balboa. "For example, lynx shifters are known to be the most vicious fighters. Razor sharp claws and fangs make them devastating hunters. Often, they are more tactical than lycan and bear kin who are their closest rivals. They tend to think about how they attack more, showing more restraint than many others."

Okay. That would have been... Davis, Jak, and Petra. Right?

The teacher continued, "For the most part, lycan are slightly taller than lynxes but less heavily muscled, so their overall size is very similar. They have claws as well, but not nearly as sharp and long as the lynxes. Their jaws are much stronger though and can crush bone easily. Less restraint and control than Lynx but more than Bear kin make them strong middlemen."

Lycan. The girl from the library. Did I know any other

lycans? My gaze swept over the class. Remmy Smith, I was fairly certain was a lycan alpha. So was the SSD teacher, Michael Watts.

My gaze was ripped back to the front of the room when Professor Balboa started talking again, stating, "On the other hand, bear kin are almost always incredibly tall and broad. They are the most violent among our shifts and tend to have the least amount of control. Their bodies are hardy, but this lack of control often puts them in a bad spot."

I was a bear kin. So was the girl next to me. My uncle. I thought that my father must have been one too, though no one had said as much.

"Avian have wide wings and are capable of both short flight and gliding. The hooked spurs on their wings can be deadly, and their beaks are for gouging. They can be very dangerous, but their more delicate bodies and hollow bones make them only offensive shifters. Cautious and thoughtful, they tend to have one hundred percent control of their faculties when they shift," continued Professor Balboa.

I hadn't gotten to know any of the avian shifters. I was going to have to change that.

He finished this section of the lecture by stating, "Then there are the saurians, like myself. We tend to be shorter, powerfully built. The shortest of all but capable of physical strength to rival the lycans or lynx. We are incredibly fast and powerful but tire quickly, with low stamina due to a saurian metabolism."

There was a pause, as he waited to see if anyone wanted to ask any questions.

When they didn't, the professor said, "Which is something every shifter has. Our metabolisms changed the moment that our shifter sides awoke. We now crave certain things. Omnivorous, and carnivorous – we crave things that we might not have enjoyed before. Many of you will likely have been privy to the new urge to hunt and eat raw meat, along with an increased appetite and hunger."

He continued to talk about the way that our appetites would have shifted, but that was something that I had already discovered on my own. My thoughts drifted briefly back to the deer that I had caught in the woods outside of my uncle's house, and the way that Petra looked when she came back into the grounds after her own hunt.

It was strange. So much had changed since I came here. It was like I had walked out of one world and into another. Like I had started a totally different life.

Some parts weren't that bad. I was stronger now. Faster, too. I had more control over my shift than most of my other classmates and if my uncle was to be believed, I was someone pretty important, too. The kind of guy that people would want dead, just because of a position I had been born into.

That probably should have made me nervous, but it didn't. I was mostly just settled into it.

Professor Balboa said, "This is just one of the many instincts that you'll have to learn to deal with as we progress through the school year. Hunger is going to be one of the easiest. At our next class, we'll discuss houses – but we're also going to be making up our first essays of the year today."

A collective round of groans went through the crowd.

The professor made a strange, reptilian clicking sound in his throat. When he blinked, it was with a second eyelid. "None of that. This is a school. Did you really think that I was going to let you sit in my class, ignoring my lectures, and not force you to own up to it? No. I want you to select a renowned shifter from your own phenotype and write a two-page essay on them. You have three days to write this in. There are plenty of resources in the library on the grounds for you to use."

More groans rippled through the class, but I was honestly a little bit excited about the prospect of doing something normal. Essays had always been a strong suit of mine. I had gotten great grades in school, but I had gotten even better ones in law school before I dropped it for the Apex Academy.

And it might even give me a chance to speak with the lycan shifter in the library and find out what she was always reading over, too. The professor continued to drone on his lesson for the next twenty minutes, but he was mostly covering the various physical changes that a first shift could bring, such as the added height and weight.

That was something I already understood and didn't need to pay too much attention to. The class was let out in due time. I was one of the last people to leave the room. I'll be honest, it was mostly because I was checking out Cass's great ass.

There wasn't any harm in looking, right? She walked in a way that made it clear she *knew* people were checking out her curves. I was pretty sure that she knew I was eyeing her up.

Unfortunately, our paths split ways pretty fast. I didn't have anything else going on until the evening, so I headed outside, letting myself meld into a bear form as I went. Loping across the school grounds, I relished the feeling of strength and power that swept through me.

And when I hit the tree line, I took off at a run.

12

Four months into classes, I had finally started to get my groove with things.

Lessons were still challenging, at least the ones that took place in the classroom. We were learning about the history of all five of the Houses. They were the big packs. The massive groups that every other smaller pack belonged to. Each house had been founded by one of the original shifters.

Trying to get the information that I needed to write essays comparing the special abilities of a lynx shifter with a saurian shifter was a pain in the ass. I was in the library late at night most of the time and found myself with less and less attention to spare for my hobbies – like playing on my MMORPG, or taking the time to read actual books for fun.

It was harder than law school.

I knew all of the terms in the university back home. Here? Totally different. Some days, I still felt like a fish out of water, grasping to try and make sense of the new instincts that sat inside of my chest, or the way that the world seemed brighter.

It wasn't just the history classes, either. The stuff that had to do with enchantments? That was still Greek to me. Literally. And if my mind wasn't filled down with how you could use alchemy to change the chemical foundation of a rock, then my body was weighed down with the physical lessons that we were being taught.

My back was pretty much always sore, and my thighs weren't much better. According to the teachers – and the other students – that was just what happens when you're first learning how to shift.

We changed our forms at least once a day no matter what classes we were in. I'll be honest. I changed mine more than once a day. The biggest benefit to having my own room in the alpha wing was the fact that I could step out of it in the middle of the night, make my way down the halls, and then change into a bear kin form when I hit the courtyard.

There was nothing better than being able to run through the woods at night.

I might have been a bear kin and not a lycan, but having the moon above me still filled me with a sort of strength that I didn't understand. A part of me thought that was because I was the prime alpha. Aaron said that eventually, I would be able to change into all of the different shifts. So, I guessed that there were latent instincts in me that matched each form.

Whatever the cause, the night was my favorite time to change. The air was cleaner. The world might have been quieter, but it wasn't empty. Owls were in the trees. I could see their golden eyes watching me carefully as my lumbering form picked its way through the undergrowth. I could smell the mice and the shrews. Somewhere distant, there was a colony of bats. Their fighting sounded like a strange, monstrous beast.

We didn't have bats in the city. At least, not anywhere that I had ever seen them.

Despite my massive size, their sounds were still unnerving. I always tried to go the other direction from them.

Making myself go back to the Academy was always hard. I wanted to stay in the forest. It called out to a feral part of me, trying to insist that I didn't leave. But I was smarter than my instincts, and I always returned to the dorm.

Eventually.

Today, I wish that I hadn't.

History And Lore is my least favorite subject. It's got nothing to do with Professor Balboa. My interest in sitting and studying has just gradually been replaced by a more powerful interest in being active. I took my normal seat, right behind Petra.

She glanced at me over her shoulder, offering me a small smile.

I smiled back at her, showing my teeth. It made her laugh.

Professor Balboa let everyone finish filing into the room. Once everyone was inside, he gave a single sharp clap of his hands. The saurian shifter was very hard on his students, but it was obvious that he really did want the shifters to do well for themselves. He cared about the students and was always trying to make sure that they had the tools they needed to succeed.

"Alright, everyone," said Professor Balboa. "We're going to cover a few things today that are very closely intertwined with each other."

Someone asked, "Aren't we going to keep discussing the phenotypes?"

"Not today," said Professor Balboa. "If you still have questions on phenotype differences, then you're going to need to check a book out at the library or see me after class. We're discussing something more important, especially as the weather will soon be changing."

That caught my attention.

What did the weather have to do with anything?

Professor Balboa turned to the chalkboard behind him and drew a circle on it. He drew two lines through the circle, splitting it into four triangles. Each one was labeled with a different season: spring, summer, autumn, winter.

"Right now, we're firmly here." He drew a line through the autumn slice. "Heading towards winter, and then spring. Come spring, you're going to be dealing with a surprisingly large problem."

Okay, consider me interested.

So far, everyone has spoken about shifting as the ultimate ability. They loved to talk about how it made us better than normal humans. Even in that, there was a serious power difference between how 'great' it was to be an alpha and the 'unfortunate' shifters who were nothing more than betas.

To actually hear a teacher talk about a downside to shifting, well, it made the whole situation seem a lot more realistic.

Professor Balboa continued, "Let's do a quick review of our rankings. I know that we've already discussed this once, but I want to make sure that we're all on the same page. The Prime Alpha is at the top, but there is an intricate ranking for alphas within the house system. Elder Alphas serve as the teachers, and while they still maintain their ranking, they are no longer young enough to breed and are instead dedicated to helping the younger alphas find their life mates."

"That's what the teachers do, right? Serve as Elder

Alphas," Petra asked. She had one arm braced against the desk, the other twisting the bright pink glitter-covered pen between her thumb and pointer finger.

Professor Balboa nodded. "Precisely. Apex Academy teaches the other students how to become 'proper' alphas for their shifts; the goal is to ensure that the alphas will know how to handle themselves within shifter society. And one of the most difficult things that a young shifter alpha has to handle is... Rut."

"Rut." I said, frowning. "Like – a deer?"

I knew that deer did that. They went into rut, which was like breeding season, and it was also when they shed their antlers. Bear kin didn't have anything to shed, far as I could tell. I supposed that the saurian might need to shed scales like a snake but... Honestly, that didn't make much sense.

"Close to it," said Professor Balboa. His mouth curled up into the barest attempt at a smile, as though my comment had greatly amused him. "Rut is the counterpart to heat. Males go into rut, and females go into heat. This allows them to better attract and breed their mate. To breed a strong shifter is the most glorious thing that an alpha can do for their house."

Breeding.

Aaron had talked about that, too. That I needed to find a mate and breed her fast, to try and get a prodigy that would take over the house as Prime Alpha if something happened to me. I knew from what Aaron said that it wasn't even just the other houses that were trying to take me out.

I had a cousin inside my own house that wanted to be the prime alpha. Aaron said that the guy would put a knife in my back if ever given the chance.

Apparently, just because the prime alpha is at the top of the food chain, that doesn't mean everyone has to listen to me on an innate level. Though the Elder Alphas are supposed to follow the prime alphas, this is a societal ruling and not an instinctual one – allowing the traitor that culled my father to work with House Blackstone.

Professor Balboa drew something else on the board, marking the triangle for spring with an X. "This is the season of breeding. Rut and heat are both beneficial to society, but they are intensely difficult to handle. If someone without a mate enters heat, they will find themselves desperate to the point of allowing anyone to breed them."

Something stirred in my chest. Interest. Heat under my skin. A flaring of – something.

One of the other students breathed out, "About time we actually talked about something interesting."

The guy behind him snickered. One of the girls nearby shot them both a sour look, and gave them a firm sounding hush, complete with a finger to the lips and wolf ears pinned back to the rest of her hair.

Professor Balboa turned back to the class, sitting the piece of chalk on his desk. He stepped around the end of it and pressed a single hand to the surface of it. His bright red scales caught in the overhead light, shiny and reflective.

The professor explained, "Males who are undergoing rut become mindless. They are focused on a single thing. Getting a mate. Because of this, it is not only important that you have a breeding partner during the season, but you must be prepared for it. Heat can last anywhere from three days to a week."

Professor Balboa was being clinical in his explanation, the way any good teacher should. But it was causing something to stir inside of me. An interest in breeding someone that hadn't been there before. I couldn't stop thinking about-

Petra.

My gaze was locked onto her back. The slopes of her shoulders under her jacket. The flash of bare throat was visible. The way that she smelled like a freshly baked peach pie. She smelled like something else, too.

Something muskier. Something enticing.

My mouth was watering. I ran my tongue over my teeth. They were sharper than they should have been.

Professor Balboa continued, as though he wasn't bothered by the way that the atmosphere in the room had changed. "To ignore your heat can be painful. To ignore your rut can be dangerous. Though we have the same innate, instinctual desire to breed as our animal counterparts, it must be noted that we are NOT animals. That is to say, we have laws and rules, and we must follow them. It is imperative that even in your most brutally basic state of mind, you maintain your humanity."

The lecture continued, telling us that as it drew closer to spring, and our first ruts and heats, more coping tips would be provided. The lesson itself wrapped back around to shifter society laws, to the concept of claiming a mate, to the idea that outside of the prime alpha, one must only breed with someone from their own shifting phenotype.

I... Tuned a lot of it out.

I knew it wasn't the right way to handle the class. It wasn't how I used to handle my classes. I was valedictorian in high school. I was acing all of my college courses. A real studious kind of guy. Something about being here at Apex Academy was changing me, though.

It was as though there was a bug in my ear, trying to push me towards the more natural reactions and responses that a prime alpha was meant to have. The common sense that I had always relied on was slipping away day by day. I was more impulsive. I was less studious. The idea of ending every issue with a fight seemed ridiculously appealing.

I wasn't the same person.

I was someone that could handle themselves in a fight. Someone that didn't back down. And judging by the boner I was sporting, someone that really, really liked the idea of breeding Petra. Maybe it wasn't just breeding. It was the idea of claiming her. Taking her as mine. Making sure that no one else would bother her.

That she would spend her time with me.

Someone questioned, "Why does the prime alpha get to breed outside of his shift type?"

"That's a good question," said Professor Balboa. "The prime alpha is meant to be part of each phenotype, to connect with them and guide all those in their house. The easiest way to form that bond is to take a mate of each phenotype. The prime alpha is also far more capable of breeding someone. Strong, good genes, and a duty to ensure that their house continues no matter what."

Someone else said, "It's because they can take on every shift."

Professor Balboa nodded. "Exactly. This means that they can breed into each pack phenotype and form a more cemented bond. It also allows the prime alpha genes to pass through different family lines, ensuring that one shift does not maintain superiority over the others. There are equal chances that a child from any breeding session with a prime will end up holding the prime genes."

This meant that if I had a kid with a saurian, an avian, or a lycan, there was a chance that any of those phenotypes would end up being the next prime alpha after me.

I had already heard this lecture. Aaron gave me the full down low on what was expected out of a prime alpha before

I came out here. It was one of the only things that he had gone into any detail on. I guess he wanted to make sure that I understood the importance of it.So the rest of the class, I let myself stare at Petra, and mostly zoned out.

She left first. I couldn't find her in the crowd. That was probably a good thing. She had gotten under my skin, but I didn't actually have anything to say to her. I wasn't going to be a creep about this shit.

Instead, finding myself in need of a serious distraction, I went back to my dorm room and I slid into the chair of my desk. I pulled up my laptop and logged into my game, a little amused by how much more fitting my username seemed to be these days. I really was a real life Shadowclaw.

There were a few PMs waiting for me, most of them from my usual buddies. But I also found myself with a new friend request. I clicked on it, a little surprised. My recent swath of inactivity had me dropping in the ranks. It seemed strange that someone would pick now to request this.

Then again, maybe it was a new player? Someone that had seen my high level and just sent out a request out of sheer hope? That had happened a couple of times in the past.

Their bio loaded up. HAWKTALON was the guy's username. He was a mid-class player, a bard class, with an enchanted bow that came from a pretty seriously difficult quest line. That was an impressive weapon.

So, not a new player. He would know that my rank had dropped by four rungs this past month, and eight since the university classes started up. He still wanted to send me a request though, huh? That was something.

There wasn't any harm in accepting the request from him. I accepted.

13

Professor Naomi Anders was a hard ass.

She was strict, she was loud, and she was powerful. Despite the fact that lynx shifters weren't innately jacked, Professor Anders had the kind of muscles that made it clear she spent all of her time outside, working hard, and training even harder.

Rather than the professional uniform that most of the other professors wore, Professor Anders wore a tight-fitting black tank top and a pair of short, black mesh sports shorts. They had a layer of tight fabric that clung to her thighs, and then the mesh hanging loose over the top of it.

She taught our shifter battle classes. Her gaze was sharp. She seemed to have something out for me, personally. Was she one of the professors that knew I was the prime alpha? There was no way to just outright ask her about it, but I couldn't think of any other reason why she was always singling me out.

Just like now."

"Victor, up front," said Professor Anders. Her voice was sharp and left no room for argument. I stood up and moved to the front of the crowd. We were on the battlefields, which looked a bit like a track field, with several large posts scattered around to mark various sections of the field.

She looked over the crowd. No one else was consistently picked for this sort of thing. It was obvious that she needed another person for the class.

"I can take him, professor," said Jak, stepping forward. He looked way too confident in himself. Just the sight of the guy had a growl building up in the back of my throat.

"Knock it off," said Professor Anders. "I want your tempers on a leash, boys. Get out here, Jak."

The other boy joined me at the center of the field.

Professor Anders called out, "Everyone else, behind the white line."

There was a white chalk line on the ground, in a large circle. This kept the fighters from spreading too far out of their designated zone and made sure that no one else got pulled into it. The other students did as they were told, stepping backwards and away from the circle on the ground.

Professor Anders did a sweep to make sure that none of the other students were inside the white line. Then she gave a sharp nod and turned back towards Jak and I.

"Alright," she said, her voice firm. "I don't want either of you going for the throat. We're not looking to have a death on our hands today. It's a practice spar. You hear me?"

"Yes, ma'am," I said. Jak echoed the sentiment, but I didn't like the look on his face. The other guy was just too... Wild.

"Alright then," said Professor Anders. She took a step backwards. "Let's get this started. Shift on the count of three. Whoever's fastest makes the first move. The fight goes until first blood is drawn, or I say to stop. And boys, when I say stop, I mean *now*."

We both made another round of agreement.

Professor Anders began the count. "One."

I could feel my muscles bunching up beneath my skin, the way that the heat rushed through me. The way it filled my head and made me lust for a fight.

"Two."

Jak took a step backwards. His upper lip curled back, showing off his teeth. They were sharp. So were mine. We were both barely keeping our shifted forms in check.

"Three!"

And just like that, we were moving. My shifted form ripped out of me with a massive roar, my body shifting into the lumbering bear kin shape faster than it had ever done before. This was the first time that I had ever seen Jak shifted. The guy was big, a six-foot red furred spotted lynx, with a snarl that could make someone's blood curdle.

We didn't have time to look each other over, simply launching towards each other. The first blow was just stupid. We slammed into each other and then bounced off. I dropped backwards, circling him. My massive paws churned up loamy soil. I twisted, throwing my body to the left.

Some of the moves were natural and innate to me, instinctive motions that a shifter should know in a fight. A lot of them had been taught to me over the last few months. Jak had a leg up on me, though. He was from a shifter family. That meant he had been watching shifters spar with each other his entire life.

I had only recently realized that the shifter society existed.

It might not have seemed like a big deal, but it meant that Jak had seen other bear kin in fights before, and I had never seen a lynx shifter in a row with someone. He knew what I could do, and I didn't know about his go-to instinctive moves.

It put me at a disadvantage.

I managed to knock him down, but his red fur was too thick and my claws didn't break skin. I roared, managing to pin him on his back, beneath me. Jak's powerful hind legs kicked out, scraping over my tender belly. I threw myself backwards, rearing up onto my hind legs.

Jak took advantage of the motion and slammed into my hindquarters, knocking me down. I hit the ground on my side, the wind knocked from me. Jak snarled and lunged – going for my throat!

Before I could even get my legs back under me, there was a second growl. Professor Anders, shifted into the form of a great, scarred lynx, slammed into Jak, and knocked him out of the way.

Jak shifted back into his human form. I dropped into mine as well. Professor Anders stayed changed into a cat for a moment. The Elder Alpha stalked towards Jak. He might have won the fight, but he broke the rules by going for the throat.

She snarled at him. Jak ducked his head in submission and stared at the ground. Once the professor was certain that he had learned his lesson, she shifted back into her human form, too.

"Both of you, get your asses back behind the white line. We're not going to have any more sparring if you little rats can't listen to me," snapped Professor Anders.

We both retreated. My belly was sore where his paws had dug into me, but there were no bruises left behind.

I found myself standing in the crowd next to another bear kin. Montague Blue, better known as Monty, was a massive guy even when he wasn't shifted. He was almost six foot five, and he was built like a brick wall, a solid chest, and broad shoulders, with arms big around as tree branches. The guy was a beast, but he was pretty fun to hang around, too.

I had been partnered with Monty in a couple of other classes, mostly our Enchanted Artifacts lessons. He was a cool guy to hang out with.

"Nice fight," said Monty. "You're getting better at controlling your temper when you shift. We've got it harder than most people do, you know. Our shift's an angry one."

I pressed a hand to my chest. The anger was still thrumming inside of me, like the twanging of a guitar string. "I've noticed."

"My dad, he's got a real hot streak. Even now. But you've got a good head on your shoulders," said Monty, with a sniff. "You've got a look about you. A smell."

"I think that's just the sweat." I wiped my forehead off with the back of one hand. "I can't wait for it to start getting cooler."

It seemed like I was always hot these days.

Monty just nodded though, clearly agreeing with me. There were damp spots under the arms of his jackets. "We run hot. The avians and saurians are lucky that they don't."

"No talking," snapped Professor Anders. Her gaze narrowed when she realized that I was one of the guys running my mouth. I gave her what I hoped would be an apologetic smile.

She didn't seem impressed by it, but she went back to the lesson, lecturing on the importance of being able to control the instinctive urge to kill during a fight. It was vital to listen to her. Jak, clearly, was not being praised for his battle tactics.

I gave Monty a glance, and he looked more amused than

anything else. Neither of us had anything to say to each other after that, opting to just stand there and listen to what Professor Anders had to say. The woman knew her shit when it came to this kind of thing, that's for sure.

When the lesson ended, Monty clapped me on the shoulder and led me away from the class grounds. We were going to get something cold to drink together from the lunch hall. He said, "Jak's an ass. You shouldn't pay him any mind."

"Yeah, I noticed that he's kind of a shit," I said. "I don't know what his problem is."

"I don't think that anyone does. The guy's weird. I used to know him when we were younger. He's an old family, you know? And he used to be an alright guy. But after we got to the Academy..." He trailed off and shook his head. "He turned into some kind of big shot alpha. He's just trying to throw his weight around and impress the ladies."

"It's not working," I said, dryly. "I don't think that anyone's impressed by him."

We stepped into the lunch hall. There was a woman standing near the entrance, leaning against the wall as she sipped at a can of soda and flipped through a book. Monty turned and made a bee-line towards her, the moment that he caught wind of her.

"Bree," he said, excited. I realized that it was the lycan girl that I often saw in the library. "I was wondering where you were. You didn't show up last night."

She gave him a smile. "Sorry. I got caught up reading." Bree gestured at her book. "And by the time I realized that the library was empty, I mean, it was like two in the morning."

"I don't know how you can spend so much time cooped up in there," said Monty, with a shake of his head.

"I get antsy just trying to make my way through study hall."

"I like it," said Bree. "And you hear all kinds of things when you're in the library. The books keep great secrets, but my ears don't."

Her ears twitched.

Monty asked, "You heard something?"

"Rumor is, Mikel is on the campus," said Bree, like that was a huge deal.

I frowned. "Who's Mikel?"

It wasn't a name that I recognized.

Monty said, "Mikel Nazzarov. He's the prime alpha of House Renoire. They're based in Austria, but they have a huge amount of control in Europe and Russia."

Bree said, "They have a huge amount of control everywhere. They control a big part of the world's economy. Even if they don't want anyone to know."

"She likes conspiracy theories," said Monty.

Bree protested, "It's not a theory. They really do control it. Mikel is one of the richest people in the world, and he's one of the most powerful, too. They used to be allied with House Blackstone, but ties were severed in recent years. No one's told us why. Like, us as in the public, and not us as in, you know, the students."

I frowned, thinking that over. "Why... Would he be here at Apex Academy?"

That didn't make any sense to me. Judging by the suddenly serious look on Monty's face, it didn't make any sense to him, either.

"I don't know," admitted Bree. "But there's no way that he has shown up here for anything good. I think that something big is about to go down, Monty. And I think that we all need to be very, very careful."

14

Aster Jones was a year older than Petra, three inches shorter, and filled with so much anger that it was a surprise her clothes weren't always stained with blood. Her knuckles were often blackened from throwing punches, though, and she was presently sporting a bandage on her cheek from where she had taken a nasty hit during a schoolyard scrap the day before.

Apex Academy didn't encourage fights among the students, but they didn't discourage it either. The new generation of shifts had to be able to form their own allegiances, and they had to be able to make themselves stand on their own. While the teachers did their best to prevent these fights from turning into something truly wild and unhinged, they didn't have too much to say about anything else.

I thought that most of the fights that Aster got into were actually about her friend, instead. Petra was a quiet sort of girl, for the most part. She didn't like getting into fights, but she was drop dead gorgeous. People were always hassling her and throwing a fit, bothering her, trying to convince her to go out with them.

Or like Jak, they were just trying to make shitty comments about knocking her up and claiming her for themselves.

I caught sight of them from across the courtyard. Aster, leaning against one of the big chestnut oak trees, and Petra next to her. Jak had seemingly abandoned his goal of getting with Petra for the time being, and was instead leaning up against Aster's side, trying to get her to pay attention to him.

I couldn't hear what they were saying. There was too much distance between us and the wind was blowing in the wrong direction. But I could see how uninterested they looked in the guy. Petra's ears were pinned back against the curve of her skull, and she was looking pretty much everywhere but at him.

Jak either didn't notice the lack of interest, or he didn't care.

It was more likely the latter of the two.

Monty said that he used to be a good guy, but I had my doubts. I figured that sometimes, being around someone since childhood was enough to alter your perception of them. Monty probably had a lot of great memories of Jak from when they were younger, back before Jak was around a ton of pretty women.

Now he had turned into a real horn dog, always trying to find someone that would mate with him.

His pickings were slim, considering that alphas could only breed with the shifters in their same class phenotype. I thought that he came across as desperate, but maybe it was just that I hated seeing him chase Petra around.

Suddenly, she reached over and tapped Aster on the

shoulder. Petra pointed towards me once she had her friend's attention, a soft looking smile on her face.

I smiled back at her and gave her a wave.

Petra and Aster spoke about something, their heads together, and then they turned and started towards me. It was still impossible to hear what they were saying, but I could see the way that Jak started to sputter. And then he caught sight of me, and his eyes narrowed. Jak's upper lip curled back, revealing his teeth.

Instinctively, my lip curled back and mirrored the look. It sent the two girls into a fit of giggles as they got closer to me. Petra asked, "Got something in your eye? You're squinting."

I rubbed my face and schooled my expression. "No, I-"

Aster was suddenly pressed right up against me, curling one hand around my arm. In a low voice, she said, "We're going to lay all over you, and you're going to be a total gentleman about it, you hear me?"

"Uh, sure?" I lifted my arm up, wrapping it around Aster's shoulders.

Petra leaned against my other side. She smelled divine, and the heat of her body against my ribs was enough to make my heart skip a beat. I curled an arm around her shoulders too, but was far more protective in the action.

It was probably majorly obvious to both women that I had a thing for Petra, but that didn't seem to matter at the moment. Their only goal was to piss Jak off by fawning all over me, and totally ignoring him.

And you know what? I was more than happy to play along with them. Leading the girls away from this section of the courtyard, we started down the hall towards the library. I wanted to use the big computers on the upper floor to check my game out. It led us straight past Jak, too.

I made sure to stare straight at the guy as we walked past him. Our eyes locked. He snarled, low in his throat, and then turned on his heel and stalked off. The girls were able to keep their composure until we made it to the walkway outside of the library. Then they both lost it, bursting into a near hysterical sort of laughter.

The two girls shook their heads, their ears twitching.

"God, that was good," said Petra, with a snort. She reached up and adjusted her hair, tucking it around her protruding lynx ears. "I think that might have been the best idea that I've ever had."

"Alright, I'll give you that one," agreed Aster. She turned towards me, looking me over. I could tell that she was judging me, trying to figure out if I was good enough for her friend.

I wondered if I was measuring up to her incredibly high standards or not.

"You did pretty good, too," Aster said.

Petra told me, "Sorry for getting you involved. I was just really sick of listening to him."

"That kind of talk's not going to land him a mate," said Aster, with a roll of her eyes. "This isn't the eighties anymore."

"It sounds more like he's come from the fifties," Petra responded.

"It sounds like he's a dick," I told them both, and that got them all laughing again. Neither of the girls wanted to go up into the library. I didn't blame them. It was a gorgeous day out. More than anything, I wanted to change into my bear kin form and take off into the forest for a run.

The thing was, I had come to realize that I couldn't let this role as prime alpha overtake my whole life. It was going

to be hard to maintain any kind of balance, but I needed to
make sure that I at least gave it a shot.

Life couldn't just be fighting and fucking, right?

So, I went into the library and up to the computers. I
logged into my account and had only been playing for a few
minutes when there was a gasp behind me.

"No way," said a male voice.

I turned to look.

Oliver was an avian delta. I had never spoken to him
before and we didn't have classes together, but I was trying
to memorize the names of as many people in the Academy
the better. The more that I knew, the safer I was. Right?

"What?" I asked.

"You're Shadowclaw?" Oliver said, a note of awe in his
voice. He was tall and lean, but not in a way that I found
particularly intimidating. I wasn't sure if that was just
because he was an avian shifter, or if it was my natural
response to a delta.

He had ropy muscles. Yellow feathers were mixed in
with his blonde hair, tinged same color as their plumage.
When he spoke, I caught sight of his teeth, which were
arranged slightly different, all pointed inward and sharp like
a bird's beak. There were more feathers around his temples,
at his elbows, and I was fairly certain that there were
feathers elsewhere under his clothing, too.

"Yeah? What of it?" I asked him, glancing back at the
screen. "You play?"

"I sent you a friend request last week," said Oliver. "I'm
Hawktalon."

He grabbed one of the other chairs and pulled it closer
to where I was sitting, turning it around so that the back was
facing me and then sitting in it backwards. He shoved a
hand towards me.

Even though he was the one that offered me his hand, he still looked surprised when I took it. I knew that a lot of people, even among the students here, treated the deltas differently. They were the lowest on the food chain, and they were often looked down on with nothing shy of disdain.

Maybe it was just because I hadn't been raised that way, but I didn't get it.

There was nothing outright different about the guy, past the fact that he wasn't as strong in a fight and he wasn't as fertile for breeding. I had no problems shaking his hand. Especially since he was a fellow gamer.

"What are the odds?" I asked, cracking a smile.

The smile seemed to put Oliver at ease around me. "I don't know. I can't believe I found someone else out here. It seems, uh, pretty wild. And Shadowclaw himself! What a name."

"It's more fitting now than I ever thought it would be," I told him. "You haven't been playing for long, right?"

Oliver's shoulders bounced. "I've been playing on and off since the site was in beta. I just can't keep consistent with it."

"I get that. I've been having the same issue. This Academy really takes up your whole life, huh?"

"Shifting takes it up," said Oliver, with an agreeable nod. He paused, and then gestured over his shoulder, towards the stairs. "I was actually heading out. I'm going to meet my sister, Isa. Did you want to come along?"

I had just sat down, but – Isa wasn't someone that I had been formally introduced to. And none of my other friends were online or available for a raid or a quest at the time. I tapped a few commands onto the keyboard, setting my character into a default training method, and then signed out.

"Sure," I said. "She's not going to mind the company?"

Oliver might have been an avian shifter, but his head popped up like a dog that had just been complimented. The guy jumped to his feet, nearly knocking over the chair. I winced. It was loud in the library. He winced too, a hand snapping out to steady the chair before it could topple over and totally hit the ground.

"Oops." Oliver rubbed the back of his neck. He seemed nervous. I wondered if he had always been that way, or if that was a developed bit of anxiety due to his ranking at the Academy. "And no, no, she's not going to mind at all. Isa loves people."

"Yeah? But is she going to mind, you know? Me?" I asked. The alphas and the lower ranks didn't mix very often.

He paused, like he had just thought about that, and then shook his head decisively. "Yeah, she's not going to mind. It'll be cool. She's going to think that you're really cool."

Really cool, huh? That was the kind of compliment that a guy just couldn't take lightly. Especially in this situation. I got the feeling that cool was the highest compliment I could get from Oliver. He looked like he really prized the concept of being seen as cool.

"Then lead the way," I told him, and let him guide me towards the stairs and out of the library. It looked like I would be starting to add a few more names to the list of people that I knew. With any luck, I would be able to add them to the list of people that I could trust to have my back in the future, too.

15

History class again, and I was stuck sitting and listening to Professor Balboa talk about the fact that the houses have always had tension. That the tension has grown in recent days. I already knew this. That's why my father ended up dead, after all.

Professor Balboa said, "House Ghadeer, of India, has their main headquarters – their school, if you wish to view it that way – in Delhi. However, they have a great reach, and they can be found even in China! These shifters have been rather conservative in their attempts to broaden the reach of their house, but they are dangerous enemies if you cross them. They put most of their efforts in defense, secrecy, economic power, and independence."

I jotted it down in my notebook, shorthand, and absently tried not to stare at Cassandra, who was sitting beside me.

"House Amin has their main headquarters in Egypt. They have control over all of Africa and are still thriving on the troves of gold and other resources harvested long ago.

This house was once the most powerful. It has found balance in the last hundred years, forming a large standing army and quelling in-fighting enough to maintain stability. They are trade partners with House Blackstone," continued Professor Balboa.

He took a few steps forward, closer to the chairs. His gaze flicked from student to student, trying to ensure that everyone was listening. Because many of his lectures could border on the dry side, he was always on the lookout for students that might not have been paying attention.

Professor Balboa explained, "We are part of House Blackstone, which is centered in the United States. Despite being incredibly wealthy, they are nearly at the bottom economically. Larger numbers of potential fighters keep them competitive, however, so they are essentially tied with the other houses, if less respected. Presently, in-fighting has weakened Blackstone's standing."

That sent up a round of people talking. It seemed as though even mentioning that we weren't at the top of our game was enough to have some of the others unhappy, and the professor was the victim of many foul looks.

He didn't acknowledge any of them. This was clearly not the first lecture that he had given about House Blackstone's failing standings in the economic field. He didn't mention the fact that our prime alpha was dead.

My father.

Something bitter twisted in my chest.

I didn't know the guy. I had never known the guy. But knowing that he had been killed for something like a title, it made me sick.

Not even killed.

Culled.

Like an animal.

Professor Balboa kept talking, explaining, "House Montez is the least powerful family, but has the singular most powerful fighters. They are just fewer in number due to a few wars. They are not quite allies with anyone, but no violence between Montez and Blackstone has occurred in over a century, though there is still bad blood from the war between Montez and Blackstone in the late 1800s."

Cassandra said, "My father told me that the head of Montez, Diego Vanderbluth, was talking about wanting to expand."

Silence. You could have heard a pen hit the ground.

Professor Balboa cleared his throat. "Diego Vanderbluth has made no advances into Blackstone territory, nor has there been any bloodshed between us."

"Right. Up until last month," said Cassandra. "Wasn't there a fight between a coyote shifter from Montez and a lynx shifter? The lynx died. That's what I heard, at least."

"That was an isolated incident," said Professor Balboa. "And it had nothing to do with clan differences or house politics. It was isolated and interpersonal, due to a family dispute between non-shifters related to the coyote and the lynx. They were handling matters in a way that was fully legal and legitimized."

It was weird to think that killing each other was just seen as legal. But I supposed that was a fact I needed to come to terms with. At some point, I would probably have to make that call. To figure out how fast I was willing to bring the hammer down on someone.

I would need to figure out how deeply I was willing to sink my teeth into someone's throat.

Professor Balboa didn't leave time for Cassandra to

continue talking, launching straight into the next house and explaining, "And of course there is House Renoire, of Europe and Russia, based in Austria. This house is the richest though not the largest."

I couldn't resist. I said, "I heard that the head of that house was here. On campus."

Cassandra's head snapped towards me. I had just become the center of attention.

Professor Balboa frowned. I was expecting him to be irritated or stammer over himself the same way that he had when the shifter's death had been brought up. But he didn't. He mostly just looked at me like I was stupid.

"Why would he be here?" Professor Balboa asked. He made a reptilian clicking sound, tongue to the roof of his mouth. "No, that didn't happen. Primes never visit their opposing house's schools."

That's not what Bree told me.

I didn't think that she was lying. I would have been able to smell it on her, if she had been lying.

But Professor Balboa clearly didn't know anything about it. I wondered if he knew what I really was. He didn't look at me the way that Professor Anders and Professor Blue did. He just looked at me like any other student.

And right now, he was looking at me as if I was a child that had just stated the boogie man was real.

Professor Balboa said, "I would re-evaluate who you're spending your time with. There would be no reason at all for anyone from the Renoire house to visit here." And then, clearing his throat, "Now, if I can get back to the lesson?"

"I have a question," said one of the other students. Fero Noriaga was short and stocky, with the kind of muscles that you didn't usually see on a saurian shifter. He held himself at odd angles, his blue hair and blue scales only making him seem more striking.

There was a flash of something on his wrist. A leather bangle, with a few silver charms on it. I recognized them as the logos to a few other MMORPG games. I had played a few of them over the years but hadn't really clicked into them.

Fero waited until the teacher nodded at him. "How does the prime alpha work into this?"

"As mentioned before, the Prime is not only the strongest, but has the ability to take on the many "aspects" of his shifters," said Professor Balboa. "This means that they are naturally the strongest of their house. Only certain shifters are born with the genes that allow them to take on this role. However, there have been cases in the past where no true prime was available to lead the house, and the role simply fell onto the strongest alpha in the area."

Oh.

That must have been what the people who killed my father had been trying to do. It was why it was important that I stay under wraps for now too. People would try and cull me, the same way that they culled him.

Professor Balboa continued, "These temporary heads only remain active until the next Prime is ready to become part of the clan."

Fero asked, "What if there is none?"

The professor paused. "What do you mean?"

Fero cocked his head to the side. He had a heavy accent and had to stop to think about what he was trying to say. Finally, he said, "The father is the prime. The son will become the prime when he dies."

"Correct," said Professor Balboa. "Which, along with a

truly intense rutting season, is one of the reasons why a prime alpha will take more than one mate."

Fero nodded. "But what if there is no son?"

A long pause. Professor Balboa said, "Well."

And then nothing.

He blinked. Fero blinked back at him.

Professor Balboa, sounding a little hesitant, admitted, "This has only happened once before in recorded history. The genes would shift. If the current prime is removed from the gene pool entirely, then the alphas of the house will – figure out who becomes the new prime. The strongest. The fastest. The smartest. It may take several children, but eventually, this new head of the house will have a child that has the prime genes, and the role will continue."

Which was why others were willing to cull my whole family. Even my cousins were willing to knife me in the back, according to my uncle, because they would just take on the prime alpha gene pool themselves.

Well, I wasn't planning on letting anyone kill me any time soon. And that meant I was going to have to try and figure out how to keep myself alive. But it also meant that I was going to have to try and figure out how to become a good prime.

These shifters, they were going to expect me to lead them. I would have to step up, taking on a role that I had never planned for. They were going to look towards me and expect me to make the hard calls.

Cassandra asked, "What does a prime even do?"

The corners of Professor Balboa's mouth curled up into a smile. "Everything." The word was said with so much awe in it. Even someone like Professor Balboa was impressed by the role of prime alpha. "But we don't have the time to get into that today. We're going to have to save that for another class."

The group, as a whole, let out an unhappy sound. The man finally had something that people were interested in, and he was just going to drop it?

That was a shame.

Especially because I could really go for some more information on the whole thing. I wanted to know exactly what was going to be expected from me. On one hand, I know why people aren't supposed to know that I'm the prime.

But on the other, it would be nice if the teachers could actually give me proper lessons. That would make things a hell of a lot easier to try and mentally sort through.

Our homework was passed out – picking one of the other houses to research and write a paper on – and then we were sent on our way. As I was heading out of class, I heard Professor Balboa say, "Actually, Fero. Just a moment. I wanted to speak with you."

Fero stopped. The rest of the students milled out. I did too, though I lingered in the hallway, next to the closed door. Fero didn't come out.

And he didn't come out.

And he STILL didn't come out.

A frown curled over my features. That made me think that something serious was going on. A part of me was tempted to try and lean against the door, see if I could hear anything inside. The rest of me knew that I wasn't four, and that was a stupid way to deal with things.

So, I made my way out of the hall instead, towards my next class. Petra was waiting for me outside of it. We had been talking more often lately. Just the sight of her was enough to smooth away my worry and my irritation.

"Hey," said Petra. "There you are. I was starting to think that you were going to play hooky for the lesson."

I laughed. "And miss out on seeing you?"

I didn't know if I was going to be a good prime alpha, especially because no one seemed willing to state exactly what I'm going to have to do for it. But I did know that Petra was the kind of girl that I wanted by my side in the coming days, no matter what.

16

Petra and I stayed with each other all through the Herbology class, but we had to part ways after that. It was the first that I had been called forward for another battle during our class with Professor Anders since the fight with Jak. I was actually expecting this to be some kind of a repeat of that performance, but instead, the professor looked through the crowd and found someone else.

"Alright, Monty. Come on up here. Let's start trying to see who's going to be the head alpha in each class. We need to know this before the end of the year, so everyone can learn their roles next semester. You're both bear kin," said Professor Anders. "Let's see which of you is stronger."

I wasn't thrilled about having to fight Monty. Partially because the guy was a lot bigger than me, and partially because we were pretty good friends. But he gave me one of those jovial grins of his when he joined me in the white circle, telling me, "Alright, Victor. Let's see who's got a better grip on their temper."

Professor Anders said, "We're going to do a countdown. Same rules as last time, boys, but I expect you both to listen to them. No throat hits. We're not looking to kill. We're looking to measure. Start on the count of three."

We both responded with, "Yes, ma'am," and then stepped away from each other, backing to opposite ends of the white marked ring.

Professor Anders did one more sweeping check to see if any of the other students were too close, and then stepped out of the circle herself. Just like with Jak, she started her count. "One."

As I started to gather my energy towards the shift, I began to lose my nerves. The exhilaration that always came with changing into a bear kin drowned out any anxiety. There was a certain thrill to this, to having to fight someone.

Getting to fight someone, actually. I was excited for it. This was different from the hunt. From going after a deer. But it was good.

"Two."

My mouth was watering. Monty and I slowly circled each other. The anger wasn't here, not like it was with Jak. While I wanted to win, I wouldn't be sad when Monty walked away alive.

He was a good guy.

"Three."

And just like that, he was an enemy.

We both shifted, though Monty changed with a roar. His stature as a human transferred into his stature as a bear kin, and I found myself facing down a hulking shifter that was almost double my size. But you know what people say: size wasn't the only thing that counted.

I made the first move, charging forward, only to feint out of the way at the last moment. Monty missed me. His momentum carried him forward, allowing me to take a massive swipe at his back end. My claws dug into the thick fur coating his hindquarters. It got caught up under the splits in them, thick and black.

Monty staggered but caught himself. He roared and came at me with gnashing teeth. Drool fell from his mouth in great, hot strands. It coated my fur when his fangs clamped around my leg. He had enough pressure in his jaw to break the limb, but this was a fight for learning, not for an actual position.

That wouldn't happen until our third semester, when packs were decided for real.

It still hurt. I would have a bruise when I changed back into my human form. I managed to twist around, grabbing at his neck and scraping my claws over it. The fur protected him, but I was able to wrench my limb free.

I was never going to win using brute strength. I had to be smart about this. Monty was bigger than me. He was raised by an Elder Alpha, who had taught him everything that he knew. A general for the old prime, no less!

Monty knew how to fight like a bear kin. But did he know how to fight like a lynx?

I thought back to the way that Jak had moved in my battle with him, and to the few times that I had caught sight of Petra out on a hunt. They kept low to the ground, and they used a lot more areal fighting moves than bear kin did. And that's how I was going to beat him.

The next time that Monty charged at me, I feinted left and went right. I dropped down to the ground, and when Monty swiped at me again, I rolled onto my back and kicked up! My hind legs dug into his belly. My front arms wrapped around one of his legs. I bit into him, and my teeth were sharp enough that they drew first blood!

That was it!

I had won!

Professor Anders was well trained. She caught the scent of copper on the wind and had transformed before I could even unhook my jaws. By the time that I was up on my feet again, she was shouldering between us, roaring.

Monty took a limping step backwards and made a low gurgling sound in the back of his throat. When he changed back into a human, there was blood on his arm. It wasn't a deep wound, though. I hadn't been aiming to break bone.

I changed back too, after a sharp-eyed look from Professor Anders. The taste of Monty's blood was still heavy in my mouth, clinging to my teeth. I spat it out on the ground, wiping the blood from my lips with the back of one hand.

Professor Anders waited a moment to make sure that no one tried to start the fight a second time, and then she shifted back into her human form as well, with a shake of her head. "Very good. First blood, drawn by Victor."

There was a polite round of clapping. Monty came over, shoving his hand towards me. We shook on it, and he grinned.

"Nice job," said Monty. "I didn't think that I was going to lose to you."

Honestly, I told him, "I didn't think that I was really going to win."

We made our way back over to the other students. Petra came over and gave me a hug. My arms wound around her waist, pulling her against me. I shoved my face into the side of her neck and breathed in deep, a singular inhale.

Peaches on the back of my tongue. I wanted her.

She pulled away, and I let her go. It almost made me whine, but I had the presence of mind to bite the sound back. Instead, I let her step away from me and say, "That was amazing, Victor. Where did you learn to move like that?"

"Exactly what I was going to ask," said Monty.

"I was just watching," I told them. "You." I nodded at Petra. "And Jak, too. I figured, hey, I can't out bear this big guy. I had to be smart about it."

"At least someone was smart about it," said Bree, coming over to check on Monty. She grabbed hold of his wrist and pulled it towards her, thumb against the underside of it. She tilted his arm this way and that, looking at the shallow puncture wounds. "You should have been more careful."

"Sorry," I told them both, gesturing at the wound.

Monty grinned at me, showing off his teeth. "I hope that it scars."

"Don't say that," scolded Bree, swatting at his chest. "You shouldn't hope for something like that!"

"Have you seen my dad? Scars are killer," said Monty. "That's how he won my mom over, you know. She wanted a powerful mate, and he could show that he was a great warrior."

Petra said, "I think that you should go see the nurse over that."

"It's fine," insisted Monty.

Professor Anders came over. "No, she's right. You need to go to the infirmary and make sure that gets cleaned up." She looked over the crowd. "Cassandra. Walk with Monty."

Bree said, "I can go with him."

She was ignored completely. Cassandra came over, offering me a polite little nod and then taking Monty by the hand and leading him down the path.

I asked, "What was with the look she just gave me?"

Professor Anders gave me a clap on the shoulder. It was the friendliest gesture that I had gotten out of her the entire time that I'd been at Apex Academy. "That was an acknowledgment. She's a bear kin, just like you."

"Right," I said. "But she's never given me a look like that before."

Petra pointed out, "You've never been the top bear kin before, either."

I frowned, not quite following.

Professor Anders explained, "Due to his size and his family's backing, Monty was the highest ranking bear kin alpha in your year. He had a chance to become the head alpha of the bear kin. But you just beat him. While nothing has been cemented in stone – and it won't be, until third year, mind you – you've still just out fought him."

Petra said, "That means you're the top bear kin now."

"Take the rest of the class off. That was a hard round. Go get a drink. Bree, go with him," said Professor Anders.

Petra's lower lip jutted out in a pout. I could tell that she would have rather gone with me instead, but we already had proof that Professor Anders didn't care what the students wanted. There was no chance of trying to argue with her.

The most that I could do was promise to meet up with Petra later, and then head out towards the lunch hall with Bree at my side. There was sweat dripping down the back of my neck. More than a drink, I really wanted a cold shower.

We were almost to the lunch hall when Bree asked, "Would you try and claim her?"

"What?" The only person nearby was a female avian. We weren't close.

Bree elaborated, "Petra. I've seen the way that you look at her."

My lips pursed. "She doesn't seem keen on taking a mate."

"If this is about Jak, I wouldn't let that dissuade you. She just wants someone better than him," said Bree. "It's hypothetical, anyway. You might fight like a lynx, but you're still a bear kin. I just mean, if she was your kind. Would you claim her?"

I was struck with the image of my teeth sinking into the side of Petra's neck, taking her as my mate with a claiming bite. So, everyone would know that she was my mate. I would be the only one to have her. To feel her around me. To breed her.

My mouth watered. "Yeah."

"Thought so!" Bree laughed. "It's a shame, right? That we can't do that."

"Eyeing someone that's not your kind?" I asked, just trying to get the subject changed.

She whined, as though she was unhappy that the topic had been twisted back onto her. Her ears flicked back into her mess of wild hair. "There's the dining hall! Let's go!"

Bree took off in a sudden run. She was fast. I had to work hard to catch up with her, especially since she had gotten a head start. Our feet slammed against the ground. Several deltas had to jump out of the way. Bree was determined not to stop – a dog chasing a squirrel – and I was determined not to be left behind.

By the time we made it into the hall, we were both panting too hard to carry on with our earlier discussion. It didn't matter too much, anyway.

Like she said, this didn't matter.

I might have been the prime alpha, but I still couldn't claim Petra. Not without giving my position away to everyone. For now, the most that I could do was think about it.

17

It turned out, the fact that I couldn't make an official claim on Petra wasn't that big of a block for me. Mostly because the moment that I saw her later that evening, as a lynx, prowling through the grounds in shift-practice, I knew that she had to be mine. It was this deep burning understanding that as the Prime Alpha, I could have her, and she would let me take her.

And though I couldn't just come off and claim her, I wanted to... Try something anyway, in a manner of speaking.

I waited until she shifted back into the form of a human, and then I waved her over. Her eyes were bright and glittering as she moved towards me, not hurrying but not dismissing the call, either. She had her lips parted and was breathing in deeply, as though she was scenting the air.

"You did amazing," she told me. "Earlier today, against Big Monty."

I laughed. "Big Monty?"

"Don't laugh! That's what everyone calls him!"

"I'm just glad it didn't piss him off too badly."

"He's going to make a good second." Petra fell into step beside me, and we started to make our way back towards the school itself. "Are you going to take that route?"

"I was thinking that I might." I had actually been thinking that when I was allowed to reveal my position as Prime Alpha, I would ask Monty to be one of my generals. I had been doing some personal reading in my free time, trying to figure out what would happen once I was the big shot in charge.

The generals were important.

They were basically the guys that helped me keep everyone else in line – but they were also the guys that I trusted to keep my back safe, no matter what was going on. They needed to be loyal, and they needed to be strong. They needed to be people that I could trust to never try and make a go at me, no matter what was happening.

I thought that Monty fit those vibes pretty well. He was a good man, he was strong, and he hadn't completely taken things sour when I beat him in the fight.

Petra said, a little softly, "You look like you're thinking awfully hard about something."

I laughed at her. "I might be."

"Are you going to share with the class?"

"Only if we're in a classroom," I told her. It was meant to be a joke, but Petra's eyes lit up and she darted forward, throwing open the door to an empty classroom with one hand, and grabbing onto my jacket hem with the other.

She pulled me into the otherwise empty room and let the door slam shut behind us.

I laughed at her. "Wow. Were you waiting for me to say that or something?"

"I just want to know what you're thinking so hard about," Petra teased.

It was too good of an opportunity. I moved up against her, pressing our bodies together and claiming her mouth in a fierce, burning kiss. Our lips slid over each other, her tongue in my mouth, my teeth on her lower lips. Our breath, hot on each other's faces.

All I could smell was Petra. Vanilla and peaches, like a pie, and something muskier. The earth of the forest that she had been hunting prey in earlier. I dropped a hand down to her side, shoving it up under her shirt. Her skin was warm to the touch, and she whined into my mouth.

Petra was like soft clay beneath me, easy to mold into my own wants and needs. She was pliable and soft, letting me push my other hand up under her shirt, too. The fabric bunched up in the front, revealing the stretch of her belly, and she whined, arching to try and press even closer to me.

My mouth moved down, lips and tongue on the stretch of her neck, tasting as much of Petra as I could manage. No marks. I knew that she wouldn't like that, and we would have to try and explain the tryst, too, but-

Ring! Ring! Ring!

The sound of the phone going off made me jump. I jerked backwards, looking around the room with wide eyes. Petra flushed deeply, red staining her skin.

Ring! Ring! Ring!

She fumbled with the bag at her side. The shoulder strap was stretched over her chest, keeping it from slipping off even during our vigorous make out session.

Ring! Ring! Ring!

Finally, she managed to get it out of her bag and answer it. "Hello?"

I tilted my head to the side, straining to make out the voice on the other end of the line, but couldn't catch even a single murmured word. A scowl crossed my face, irate at the fact that we had been interrupted... and even more irritated because whatever this call was, it couldn't be good news.

I hated the look on Petra's face, her brows pinching down and her lips twisting first into a thin line and then parting, as though she were exhaling. "Alright," she said, her voice soft and almost shaky. "Alright. I will."

The call ended. I asked, "What's wrong?"

Because clearly, everything was NOT okay.

Petra shook her head. She shoved the phone back into the bag. Her ears were pinned flat against the side of her head, buried beneath her hair. "It's fine. I just – I have to go."

"What?"

"I'm sorry, Victor. I have to go." Petra ducked out from in front of me, turning around and walking backwards towards the door to the classroom. She paused when she got there, and her whole body seemed to droop for a moment, her shoulders dropping, her jaw going soft.

She looked like she wanted to say something else. I would have pushed, but I didn't want that to spook her off entirely. So, I let her leave without protest – and yeah, okay, maybe that was stupid, but I was trying not to be a total asshole to her. I figured that Petra had enough people clawing all over her. She wasn't going to want jack shit to do with me, if I was the same raging prick as those other alphas.

And considering she was of the belief that our shift set was an issue, I was going to need to make sure to handle things right.

But – there wasn't any point in sticking around the empty classroom without her, either, so I turned and stepped out into the hallway. I had barely made it out of the room when hands were balling up in the front of my shirt and shoving me hard against the wall.

I lashed out on instinct, making a swipe with one hand. My claws flashed. Jak jumped backwards at the last minute, avoiding taking a hit to the face. He let out a snarl that was pure lynx, his ears pinned back.

"What the fuck do you think you're doing?" I demanded; my proverbial hackles raised.

Jak didn't back down, though he did keep his distance. Had he not been expecting me to fight back? I got strange feelings in regards to him. He tried to act like he was some kind of a big shot, but I felt like he was too rash and impatient to ever make it as a top alpha.

And this just proved my point. To start a fight and not expect that the other person was going to follow through. It didn't make any sense at all.

I bared my fangs at him and snarled.

Jak hissed right back at me. He shook his head, and he told me, "You need to back off."

"Or what?" I figured that he must have been talking about Petra. She had been the so-called apple in the guy's eye for a while. "You think that you can really make me do anything?"

"I would have killed you if the professor hadn't stepped in," warned Jak.

That was true. But it was also true that I had gotten a lot stronger since then, and smarter, too. I kept learning, and Jak already viewed himself to be at the peak of his existence. That was going to be the guy's biggest failing.

Jak seemed smug, though. He didn't realize that he wasn't powerful enough to throw his weight around anymore. He took a step towards me, just one, like he thought that getting closer to my personal space would make me less likely to challenge him.

I wasn't a dog.

I wasn't going to be cowed by some mangy cat that was too big for his own britches.

Jak bared his teeth at me. He dropped his voice down low and insisted, "You're going to back off, or you're not going to like what happens."

"Yeah? What are you going to do?" I tilted my chin back, and I tried to do everything that I could to make sure that he knew I wasn't scared of him.

Jak either ignored it, or he didn't pick up on it.

Instead, he gave another low, feline growl. The sound was almost warbling in tone, and his teeth flashed at me, a mouth filled with sharpened fangs. Saliva clung to them. Even though I wasn't scared of Jak, per se, it was still unnerving to have them so close to my throat.

"I'll make you regret it," said Jak. "You and everyone else that gets in my way."

"Everyone, huh? Seems like you're going to be fighting a lot of people," I said, but Jak wasn't listening. He must have felt like he had made his point, because with one last snarl, he turned, and he stormed down the hallway.

The sound of his shoes slamming against the tile beneath me filled the air. Irritation burned at the back of my chest. I couldn't understand why this guy was being such a prick unless he had seen me come into the room with Petra.

That was when his mood had turned south before, right? When I started flirting with her?

But that didn't seem right. Jak was a whiny kind of guy with a short temper, who thought that he was surely the gift to women that everyone in this school was waiting for. That wasn't up for debate. Whatever friendship he had been trying to piece together on my first day at the Academy had shattered the moment that I had shown an ounce of interest in the pretty lynx shifter.

I just didn't think that he would come after me so fully *just* because of Petra.

Other people had been flirting with Petra, and as far as I could tell, Jak hadn't been making threats against them. He was an ass, sure, and he didn't like to be told what to do. But he had never outright threatened them.

I was the only one that he was treating this way.

Could... Could he have somehow figured out that I was the Prime Alpha? No, that was ridiculous. He wasn't smart enough to figure it out... Unless someone had told him.

A wave of concern washed through me.

Could one of the teachers have ratted me out? If so, why would they go with Jak of all people?

There was something more going on here. I had to figure out what it was. So, though it was already late evening, and I really would have rather just gone after Petra to see what had pulled her away from me, I turned and headed towards the library, instead.

I was certain that there would be something in there about Jak's family line. He was always citing the fact that he was from an old family of shifters, right? Maybe I could use that to figure out what was really going on.

Fuck, it was at least worth the try.

18

Jakarta Reed is the oldest son of the Reed family. And yeah, they used to be a pretty big deal. The keyword there is USED to be. At some point, they were sort of big shots among the lynx shifters. They had money, they had prestige, they had a big house in the south with a ton of acreage attached to it.

But Jak's granddaddy made a couple of bad business dealings, and his *father* was born more on the sickly side, which meant that he wasn't much of a fighter. They were left without any money, with no good claims to their name, and with nothing going on but Jak.

The prodigal son.

Clearly, there wasn't anything in the library records about Jak. He was an active student, and he hadn't done anything worth being written down. But I could piece things together on my own pretty well, based off of how the history of the Reed family was looking.

It seemed to be that a lot was riding on Jak's shoulders. So, that explained the attitude at school. But it didn't explain why he had it out for me personally. I figured that he might have been working with someone, but the Reed family hadn't made any dealings of particular that were noteworthy, at least not according to the family tree books in the library.

Great Grandmother Reed had been claimed by someone named Harry Billard, an oil tycoon, but even that had just been a monetary exchange. And again, they lost pretty much all of their money one generation down. So, I was left without any actual leads. Another dead end.

Groaning, I tilted my head back, letting it hang towards my shoulders. I rocked backwards in the chair, so that the front legs weren't on the ground. I had just started to let my mind drift when-

Ring! Ring! Ring!

The sound of my phone going off nearly made me piss myself. I jerked, and the chair threatened to skid out from under me. My arms waved through the air, legs kicking out in a desperate sort of flail. I was able to catch myself at the last minute, the chair thumping back down on the floor. It was a good thing that I was up on the second level, and that it was almost ten at night, or else the librarian would have chewed my ass out over all that racket.

Speaking of-

Ring! Ring! Ring!

The phone was still going off.

"I should have muted you!" I snatched up the phone and glanced at the caller ID. I didn't recognize the number, but I answered it anyway, with an out of breath and slightly terse, "Hello?"

"Victor? Thank God. Monty said that this was your number, but I wasn't certain." Petra's voice was trembling.

I shot up onto my feet, so fast that this time the chair

behind me did skid away and hit the ground with a clatter. "Petra? What's wrong?"

"It's Oliver."

The avian delta that I had been playing MMORPG's with? A heavy frown crossed my face. With one hand, I set the chair back up. With the other, I moved to start shoving my stuff into my bag, keeping the phone tucked between my shoulder and my ear.

"What's wrong with Oliver?" I asked.

Something big. I could tell from her voice.

"He's been beaten," said Petra. Her voice caught. "We're at the infirmary, Victor. Can you come over?"

"Beaten?" My mind flashed to what Jak had said earlier, about getting rid of everyone that stood in his way. Could he have been talking about Oliver, along with me? That just made the mystery seem that much stronger. I wondered what a delta could have done to Jak.

There was no way it had been anyone else, though.

The deltas were by and large dismissed by the alphas. No one paid them the time of day, let alone cared enough to cause this kind of an issue.

"Alright, where are you?" I asked.

Petra sniffed. Was she crying? The thought made something in the back of my chest twist up. I hated the thought of her crying. I would handle any problem that upset her that badly.

"We're in the infirmary," said Petra. "I'm sorry. I didn't know who else to call."

"You have nothing to be sorry over," I told her, earnestly. "Give me four minutes. I'll be right there."

"Thank you." Petra's voice broke. She absolutely WAS crying.

I wasn't sure what this whole thing was about, but I

knew this much: I was going to kill Jak for upsetting Petra so much.

With one more promise to be there fast as I could, I got off the phone and shoved it into my back pocket. Eyeing my bag, I carried it down with me and then left it at the librarian's desk, knowing that it would just slow me down.

Without having to worry about carrying my bag, I was able to change into my bear kin form the moment that I stepped outside. There was a strict no-shifting in the library policy, in an effort to protect the books. The rest of Apex Academy was built to accommodate even the largest shifted form.

That meant, not only was I able to cross the courtyard in record time, but I was able to race through the halls of the school building itself, fast as my lumbering bear form would take me.

I didn't drop back into my human form until I was directly outside of the infirmary. I shook myself off, giving my heart a minute to stop racing, and then stepped into the room.

The infirmary looked like any other school nurse's office, though there were posters of animal anatomy on the wall, along with the standard ones about human organs and body issues. Several cots were set up on the far side of the room, each one with an individual curtain around them, to offer privacy. All but one were sitting open; Oliver must have been the only patient at the moment.

The air reeked with the tang of antiseptic, and the burn of cleaner. But beneath that, it was heavy with blood, sweat, and the salty tang of too many shed tears. My nose wrinkled at the smell. The door clicked behind me, alerting others of my presence.

From inside of the curtain came Nurse Bellsworth. She

was a short, portly woman. Everyone that I had spoken with claimed that she was a different class within shifter structure, some of them citing her as an Elder Alpha, and others claiming that she was barely above being a delta. I wasn't able to tell by scent. The cleaner that clung to her was too much, a tang of bleach that over rode everything else.

Her blouse was a little on the tight side, barely containing her breasts, and her pencil skirt clung to the swell of her hips, hanging over her thick thighs. Her blue tinged hair was pulled up into a tight bun at the back of her head, though that didn't hide her lycan ears, or the thick claws protruding from her fingertips.

"I would assume that you're here to see Mister Castaway," said Nurse Bellsworth.

I nodded. "Yeah. Is he-"

The sound of my voice was all that it took for Petra to come out of the curtains. She shoved them aside in the process. I had a brief chance to glimpse Oliver, thoroughly wrapped in blood spotted bandages, bruised and battered, on the cot, and two teachers, before she threw herself at me.

I caught her around the waist, steadying her., Petra let out an animal keen, wrapping her arms around my shoulders. She shoved her face into the side of my neck. "It's my fault!"

"It's not your fault," I told her. After a moment, she stepped away from me. I clung to one of her wrists. "What happened?"

"It's Jak," said Petra.

Professor Beaumont shook his head. "We've no proof of that yet."

"I know it was him," Petra shouted, spinning around to face him.

Professor Beaumont stepped forward, looking us both

over. His gaze lingered on me. He was a tall man, and not a
kind one, either. Sedrick Beaumont taught Arcane
Weaponry. He was one of the only beta teachers in the
Academy, and rumor had it, he was a beast on the battlefield
due to his knowledge of magic.

"An idle threat is not proof," said Beaumont.

I demanded, "Did he threaten you?"

"He said that he would ruin everything, when I told him
that I would never mate with him." Petra turned towards me
suddenly, her hands snapping out like she was desperate to
have something steady to hold onto. Her whole body was
trembling, and the fear-scent coming off of her was insane. I
had never seen her like that before. "He said that he would
claim my baby sister, just to spite me."

Anger flared inside of me. I spun to face Professor Beaumont. I demanded, "And you're just going to let that
happen?"

"We have no proof that Jakarta was involved in this,"
said the professor, dryly.

The other teacher in the room was Professor Balboa. I
would have been surprised to see him there, but the guy had
a soft spot for deltas. I was fairly certain that both of his
younger siblings had ended up as deltas, so he tried to keep
an eye on them now.

"We're looking into it," said Professor Balboa. "Our first
order of business was simply ensuring that Mister Oliver
here was going to be alright."

"He should be fine," said Nurse Bellsworth, heading
back over to where Oliver was laying in the bed. I was able
to get a better look at him this time around, and the sight
made my stomach twist. He hadn't just been beaten up. It
looked like whoever was trying to attack him had been

genuinely trying to kill him. "I have salves that can go on it. And my charm."

She wore an enchanted necklace, which gave her the ability to – something. I didn't know. I was sure that we had covered it during one of our classes, but at that moment, the facts were slipping away from me. I was too angry to pay attention to that. My rage burned inside of me, twisting higher and higher, until it was all consuming.

It didn't matter what Jakarta Reed's motives were. It didn't matter if this was really all about Petra, if it was really all about me, or if it was something else entirely. It was clear that neither of the teachers were going to handle this. Not quickly, at least, and not in a way that mattered. And that meant that someone else was going to need to do it.

That meant *I* was going to need to do it.

"Stay here," I told Petra, my voice low and rough, the growl twisting in with my words. I was so angry that I could barely contain my shift form from breaking out of my body. It was right there, beneath the surface, threatening to come out. "I'll be back."

"I'm sorry," said Petra, the word a soft, broken thing.

"Don't be," I said. She hadn't done anything wrong. "Just promise me that you're going to stay here."

"I promise," said Petra, softly. She pulled one hand up against her chest.

Professor Beaumont demanded, "Where do you think that you're going?"

But I didn't need to account to him. I hadn't done anything wrong. Not yet at least. So, with one last snarl, I turned and vanished out into the hallway. Professor Balboa called after me, but I dropped back into my bear kin form, unable to keep it at bay any longer, and ignored him.

Jak had gone too far this time. I wasn't going to stand by and let him hurt anyone else.

19

It was easy to find Jak.

Almost eleven at night. The grounds of the Academy were always brightly lit, with massive spotlights on the buildings and metal posts that contained lights, like you would find on the side of busy streets in the city. Other lights were scattered about, solar powered stones that gave off faint blue glows marked various trail heads into the forest that surrounded the academy, and several smaller spike type lights marked the sidewalks.

Though to be fair, almost all shifters had the ability to see well at night, so we didn't need as much light as a normal human did. Even aside from the lights, in my bear kin form, I was easily able to sniff him out. I could find him.

I could!

And I did.

He was standing around near the east wing, outside, at one of the stone circles. A few of his beta friends were sitting on the various stones. Jak was standing up, leaning against one, bragging. Bragging! He looked like he was having the time of his life out there, telling them all about how he had beaten up Oliver and threatened Petra's sister.

The rage inside of me was too much. I slammed myself into him, shoulder checking Jak hard. He went soaring sideways, hitting the ground and rolling. Two of the betas jumped down from their perches.

One of them, Michael West, demanded, "What the hell are you doing?"

I changed back into my human form, snarling. Spit dripped from my fangs. My whole body jerked, shoulders bouncing, and the muscles in my neck flaring and pulsing with the rage of it all.

Jak jumped to his feet. He shook himself off, throwing his body about in the process. He must have thought it made him look tough, but it didn't. "What do you think you're doing?"

"How dare you do that to Oliver?" I snarled.

"That little shit should have minded his own business," Jak told me. "It's what he deserved for getting involved in my affairs."

"Petra isn't your affair. She doesn't want you around her, asshole," I snarled.

"That was her mistake," Jak said, tilting his head back. His beta crew were growing closer to him now, looking as though they weren't entirely sure what the fight was about. It didn't matter. They were going to back Jak up no matter what.

That meant that I would need to take them all on, and not just Jak in this fight.

For a moment, I hesitated. Four against one, that was going to be hard. But then my anger swelled again, and I realized that I couldn't back down. Petra was depending on me to put an end to this, before Jak went and did something even worse.

There was no way in hell that I was going to let Petra down!

I snarled and took a step forward, my shoulders bunching, my muscles flexing. "No, Jak. This has been your mistake, and I'm going to prove it to you. I'll give you one last chance to back down, and swear that you're never going to bother Petra, Oliver, or their families ever again. One chance!"

Jak responded by shifting! His lynx form appeared and was only visible for a second before he was launching himself forward, throwing himself at me!

I snarled and threw myself to the side, rolling to avoid the attack, just like we had been taught. I sprung up onto all fours, letting the shift take over my body. Once I had taken on my massive bear kin form, I snarled and roared. Around me, the other shifters changed, too.

Betas weren't as big as the alphas in their form. Being a beta did not necessarily mean that someone was a "weak" shifter. Many Betas are strong enough to challenge the Alpha, and if one succeeds, it will become more powerful as its hormones adjust to its new rank. Male and female shifters can be Betas, and they were forbidden from breeding with anyone but other betas or deltas.

Jak's lead beta was Reese Green. I had seen him around a few times. Then there was Jessica Hamil, who was the only female beta in the group. She had a crush on Jak, common knowledge, and since they couldn't breed with each other due to the class restriction, she had taken to trying and proving her worth to him in other ways.

The third beta was – I didn't know his actual name. Everyone on campus just called him Rook. He was big for a beta, and heavily scarred for someone that was in his twenties. It was commonly thought that he had either come from a family with a dark way of working out their anger, or that he had been raised up by other shifters for the sole purpose of being a lead beta and winning fights.

I would have felt bad for the guy, if he wasn't a raging prick to everyone that tried to speak to him.

Unease over took me.

Four against one.

The three betas spread out, circling us. Jak stood several feet away, head raised and ears pinned back. He was waiting, I realized, for me to make a coward's run for things. But that wasn't going to happen.

I was no coward – and I was sick of the way that he treated Petra. I was sick of the way that he treated Oliver. And I would never let his threats of claiming Petra's sister out of spite become reality!

With a snarl, I made the first move. My bear kin form was much larger, and he was able to avoid it. My front paws had barely touched the ground when Jessica charged me, swiping out with one massive lynx paw.

I dodged the attack, but it left me unbalanced, and my body wavered. I staggered sideways, and Jak took advantage of it, lunging. This time, he got me, and we rolled across the ground, the betas moving so that they could keep circling us. Clouds of sand and dust were kicked up.

All of our yowling and snarling was starting to draw in a crowd. The others weren't allowed to fight, though. Any time someone got too close, Reese would snap at them and force them back. That would have been fine, if they were just trying to keep others out of this fight.

Instead, they were doing me dirty.

Every time that I would manage to get a handle on Jak,

one of the betas would get involved. It would be two or three against one, with the remaining beta circling us and making sure that no one else got involved.

They were fighting dirty. I would never be able to get a handle on things if this kept up!

Suddenly, Jessica was tackled from the side!

She went rolling through the grass. It was Mack O'Neil!

Mack was a big bear kin beta, and one of Monty's closest friends. I was under the impression that they knew each other even before the academy.

I turned to look. It wasn't just Mack. It was Monty, too, and three other members of his crew!

Monty had already changed form, showing off his massive bearkin body. He lurched forward with a roar, easily taking on Reese Green! The fight was on!

Now that I wasn't so out numbered, it was a lot easier for me to try and get something done. There was blood matting down the fur of my back leg from when Jessica had managed to bite me. Pain shot through the limb with every step but I wasn't deterred.

For a moment, Monty dropped back, so we were side to side. We chuffed at each other, communicating without words.

I didn't know if he had come here because Petra had called him, or if he had just heard the commotion and been drawn in that way. Either way, I was glad to have him at my side. I was fairly certain that the look on my face was able to convert that.

We didn't have long to work together, or to figure out what a plan was. We didn't have the chance for anything, really.

The fight was still on.

While the lynx betas had been taken off guard by the

arrival of Monty and his crew, they had gotten their bearings back. All three of the betas were focused on the fight now. No one was circling us, which meant that I was able to use my body to back Jak away from the rest of the group.

The goal was to separate him and fight that way, but Jak had other plans. He twisted past me and leaped onto one of the rocks behind us. His claws scoured over the stones, leaving marks behind. The stones were covered in claw marks of former students.

I wasn't much of a climber.

My form was lumbering and large. I circled the stone though, snarling and growling up at him, taunting him the best that I could. Was he just going to stay up there and hide? Was he really content letting the fight end like this?

Around me, the betas were being dispatched. Reese had been pinned to the ground by Monty. He had the back of the lynx's neck in his maw, though he wasn't biting down to kill. It was a mark of dominance, and a clear end to the fight.

The other two lynx's were quickly dispatched in the same manner, thanks to Mack and the rest of the bear kin betas.

It was just going to be the two of us now.

I snarled at him, goading him down into a fight.

Jak's ears pinned back. He looked a little concerned. Clearly, he hadn't been expecting anyone to come to my defense. He certainly hadn't been expecting the betas that followed him around to be so swiftly dispatched.

It was his own fault.

Jak thought he was the toughest lynx out there. He thought that he was the toughest alpha in the school. He wasn't. He relied too heavily on his beta crew, like in our fight so far, and even beyond that – he didn't try to improve.

If you go through life already viewing yourself as the

best, then there was no way that you would ever get any stronger. There was no way that you could ever get any more powerful.

Other people would continue to grow. They would form new allies; they would learn new techniques. I had. Not only had I managed to get Monty as an alpha who would back me in any fight – and tonight proved that – but I had been learning how to use my bear kin form to a better advantage.

Meanwhile, Jak had just been sitting there and stagnating. He didn't think that there was any point in trying to improve, because he already believed himself to be the best.

It had gotten him into a bad situation.

The betas had been removed from the fight. It had clearly shaken Jak's confidence... But a large crowd had gathered around us. Everyone was watching. Other lynx shifters, too. A few teachers were eyeing the fight from the back, trying to decide if they needed to break it up. If he backed out now, then his reputation would never recover.

Even losing the fight would be better than just running away from it. At least then, he would have a chance to get stronger, and challenge me again later. Running away from the fight, though... that was a totally different story.

I roared, shaking my head from side to side and baring my fangs. Spit flew in all directions. My heady, purple tongue unfurled from the side of my mouth.

There was a pause, a single beat of silence. Then Jak returned the sound with a scream of his own.

Finally, he jumped back down onto the ground in front of me.

The fight was back on!

20

Jak didn't lunge right away. It was clear that he was trying to strategize, since his original plan of having the beta crew nip at my heels until I left wasn't working. But I wasn't going to give him the time to think things over.

I moved first. Rather than circling him like we had in the first fight, I went straight for the side. He dodged my attack, but I kept pushing forward, rearing up onto my hind legs so that I could strike out, like a boxer.

I had Jak on the retreat. He couldn't do anything but try to avoid my blows. The crowd that had formed parted around us like water and then reclosed, making sure to stay out of our way but never letting us leave.

There was no way that I was going to let him use the stones in a fight against me. Lynx shifters were agile and fast. I was certain that he would be able to use them to get to the upper ground.

Once I had driven him far enough away from the stones that it wouldn't be a problem, I dropped back down onto all fours and tried to shoulder check him. The lynx shifter let me hit him, but he twisted around, sinking his claws into my flank.

I howled as the pain raced through me. Jak used his claws to pull himself up. He made it onto my back, but I used that to my advantage. Dropping down onto the ground, I all but rolled on top of him. My massive weight pressed down onto Jak, and he screeched as he was briefly crushed beneath me.

The roll was completed and I got back on all fours, putting distance between us. Earth was caking up between my paws and under my thick, black claws. Jak stood up and tried to shake himself off, sending clumps of dirt in all direction.

He was panting hard, drool in the corner of his mouth. I hadn't made a good enough blow, though. If I wanted to be the victor of this fight – and better yet, if I wanted to make sure that we never needed to have it again – then I needed to do something drastic.

Something that Jak would never be able to come back from.

It was strange.

I didn't think that I had ever been this angry of a person. The moment that I had undergone that first shift though, the anger had been ever present. It sat just beneath the skin at all times, shuddering and twisting, a fire that was ready to catch on to something greater and take down the whole forest.

Even now, it was there. It made my skin feel hot.

Something clicked.

The teachers said that the bear kin were some of the most aggressive. And Monty, he said that bear kin always ran hot.

I wondered if it really was a physical reaction to the

intense sensations of anger that I was feeling, to the way that the hatred and rage bounced about beneath my skin.

This wasn't the time to think about it.

Jak was moving again. He kept his body low to the ground, practically slinking in a wide circle around me. I wanted to give him even less to hit, so I rose up onto my hind legs once more, stretching out to my full, towering height.

I was over seven feet tall when I stood like this. Jakarta, tail tip to nose, was barely six foot five. That didn't mean he wasn't strong. It didn't mean that a bear kin couldn't lose a fight.

But it sure made me feel a hell of a lot of pride. It made me FEEL like it was giving me an advantage.

Some people had said that just thinking you could win, that was the most important part of a fight. Even if you were weaker, you never went into a fight thinking that you were going to lose. Having a mindset like that meant that you were never going to even have a chance.

So even though I was strong, even though Jak was strong, I had to believe that I was the best. I had to know that I would be able to win.

And you know what? I did.

It didn't even take any convincing.

All it took was thinking about the way that Oliver had looked in that bed, and thinking about the way that Petra looked when she was crying, and the rage became so much, there wasn't a single doubt in my mind that I was going to let Jak win.

I was going to crush him. He would pay for what he had done to my friends, and for what he had threatened to do. I would never let him get away with it.

So, I roared and I threw myself forward, slamming

bodily into Jak. It took him by surprise. He had been expecting me to wait. But I wasn't going to win this fight by being on the defensive. I was going to need to take him down, and do it hard, if I wanted a chance at getting Jak to back off from Oliver and Petra.

So that's what I did.

I came down on him with my full body weight. Jak bit my shoulder, fangs latching into the flesh. He bit down hard enough that I could feel the damage done to the bone, the way that it threatened to give beneath the force of his jaw.

With one massive paw, I knocked him free. He went rolling, and skidded to a stop, jerking back onto his feet. I didn't give him any time to catch his breath.

The moment that Jak was on all four paws, I was on him again. It was a constant barrage of it. One hit and then another. My claws raked through his fur and dug into his skin. My body slammed into Jak's, knocking him down.

He tried to pull the same trick on me from the fight before, where he got underneath me and kicked at my soft underbelly, but I was expecting it. I had used the same trick in my fight with Monty. It wasn't going to catch me off guard.

And he wouldn't be able to win if he couldn't catch me off guard.

It did hurt, though. His claws were sharper and longer than mine, and this wasn't a practice fight under a teacher's watchful gaze. It split open the flesh of my belly and left massive bruises behind. I managed to get away from him, kicking out with one back leg and catching him square in the side.

It didn't deter him – but it gave me an idea.

See, I couldn't just be big and strong. I had to be smart, too. That's what let me beat Monty in the fight, and it's what was going to let me beat Jak here, too.

I realized when I kicked at him that a big cloud of dirt had gone up, and Jak had to squint through it. I dropped onto my hind legs and used my front legs to scoop up massive pawfuls of the soil, sending it flying backwards, like a dog that was digging for gold.

Jak screeched and backed away, slamming his eyes shut and pinning his ears back flat against his head.

He kept reaching up with one paw, swiping at his face. While he was temporarily blinded by the sand, I spun around and went for the final blow! I knocked Jak down, and I pinned him. Then I grabbed him by the throat in my massive jaws!

His dirty fur was pressed to my tongue. The taste was awful. Drool spilled from between my fangs. I didn't bite down hard, making sure not to break the skin. This was supposed to be a threat, and it seemed to be working. Jak went totally limp beneath me. The lynx shifter had frozen. A low whine rattled out of his chest.

I could feel the way that the sound made his throat vibrate between my jaws. When he swallowed, I could feel that too; I had to be careful that the bob and dip didn't make me lose my grip or push too hard into my teeth.

A growl built out of my own chest.

Everyone was watching me.

Killing Jak now and being done with it, that was a tempting thought... But I didn't want the reputation of a ruthless killer, especially not since I was going to become the Prime Alpha later. I wanted to be respected, not just feared.

So even though I could have killed him, I let him go.

The fight was over.

I pulled away from Jak, and I changed back into my human form. It was the ultimate way of making it clear to

Jak that I didn't think he was a threat. I wasn't even leery enough to stay in my bear kin form while he was shifted.

There was grit between my teeth. I used my tongue to wipe it out, and then spat it onto the ground next to Jak's muzzle. The wounds had changed with me, though they were much smaller and less grave on my human form. I knew that they would heal fast, too.

That was the only reason why I hadn't been more concerned about Oliver.

While delta shifters might have had a much lower healing rate, they were still hardier than humans, and their bodies were able to recover at a much faster rate. Jak was lucky about that. I might not have been so concerned about my reputation if things were different.

As it was, I turned away from him, and started to make my way back towards where the others were gathered. Monty changed back into his human form, too. There was a look on his face that could only be called respect.

Sometimes, you needed to make those calls. The teachers had been very firm and explicit in explaining that shifter society wasn't the same as human society. Sometimes, a death would still be treated as a murder. This was called culling; it was what had happened to my father, though I had yet to mention that to anyone.

But in other instances, killing an alpha that had challenged you was simply a matter of pack safety, and a way of keeping your position. It was a very intricate balance between culling someone and killing them out of need, and one that only existed in the shifter world.

Sometimes, these crimes would be brought before Elder Alphas to be examined, if it seemed to be leaning too closely towards a senseless culling, or if it was a death that involved the members of two different houses – like the one near the border that had been brought up, and dismissed, in class.

However, it was mostly left to the pack to decide. If they thought that the killing was justified, then there would be no reason to try and usurp the current head alpha, and there would be no reason to look for another pack to take you in.

This could have been a fine line for me to walk. Many of them would have respected my decision, if I had opted to kill Jak... but just as many of them would have thought that the punishment wasn't worth the crime.

He thought that I had made the right choice by letting Jak live this time, too.

I nodded at him, just once. A sharp, terse motion. It was both an acknowledgment of the praise, and a thank you for the help. And then his expression changed.

Monty took a step forward. He shouted, "Victor, look out!"

I spun around-

but it was too late!

Jak, still in his lynx form, had already leaped. And he was aiming right for me!

21

Jakarta Reed was a no good, dirty, lousy cheat.

He slammed into me as a lynx, even though I was a human and even though I had already won that fight. A ripple went through the crowd. The loss of respect that such a dirty move garnered was instant. But Jak didn't seem to care about that.

I managed to get out from underneath of him, and caught sight of the look in his eye. It was almost crazed. Wild and frantic, desperate. Was this still about saving face? Something told me that it wasn't.

This was about... whatever had driven Jak into hating me so much in the first place. My proverbial hackles raised. I knew that I had to act fast. This fight had to end, before Jak did something stupid.

But when I reached inside of me for the energy to change back into my bear kin form, something else reached up and hit me instead. It was a hard, sudden snap. A push of energy that seemed to rocket through me.

It was a shift, but it wasn't the bear kin form that I had become accustomed to. It felt different. Less angry, somehow, but no less powerful. It pressed towards me, and I let it engulf me.

The change was fast, as they always were, but it was different. My muscles twisted and my bones snapped, reshaping, but not into the form of the bear that had become second nature to me. This was different. A sort of litheness took shape around me, and my fur, black and shaggy, had the faintest dapples in it.

A lynx body. That's what I had. Four paws on the ground and a short, nubbed tail behind me. Tufted ears and jaws that were so strong, they could crush bone. The silky, glossy coat was my own. This felt right. It was an extension of my own power, another skin that wrapped around my bones.

The crowd fell silent.

I realized too late that there was no way to explain a second shift. Only the Prime Alpha was able to change into more than one phenotype of shifter. That meant that there was not a person in the school that, come morning, would not know who and what I really was.

The concern for that situation was far more distant, however, compared to the one in front of me.

Jak didn't look surprised. If anything, he seemed triumphant. That proved what I had been guessing; he must have already known that I was the Prime Alpha.

Someone had told him.

But who?

There was no time to figure it out. Jak clearly wasn't going to stop and answer any of my questions. I was given no time to accustom myself to my new form before he surged towards me again. There was something different in the motions now.

Jak wasn't thinking anymore.

These were sloppy, messy strikes. It was a desperate fight, on Jak's end.

Even though I had never fought in a lynx form before, I had studied their moves. If I could do them as a bear kin, then I could pull them off even more smoothly as a lynx. It kept us on even grounds.

I might have been at a disadvantage under normal conditions. There was a reason why it was so important that we trained to fight in our shifted forms, after all. It was odd, having my limbs be in new spots, having my eye line hit a different location. I was almost off kilter.

If Jak had stopped to put even a little bit of thought into what was going on, he might have been able to win the fight. He might have been able to at least get in a few crippling blows.

But... something had changed in Jak.

He wasn't trying. Not the way that he should have been. He wasn't taking advantage of my inability to fully understand the limits and power of my new body. He wasn't aiming for killing blows.

Jak wasn't aiming at all.

A strange desperation was lit inside of him. His only goal seemed to try and make as much contact with my body as possible, even if the blows were only glancing things that took out tufts of fur instead of breaking the skin and drawing blood.

I was aware, in a distant way, that the crowd had changed. That a hush had fallen through them. Many of them were probably still trying to grapple with the idea that I wasn't just a bear kin alpha, but the actual Prime Alpha.

When this fight was over, I would have to deal with it.

For now, though, I had just seen my opening – and I was making a strike!

I threw myself forward, and I grabbed his neck in my own jaws. They were strong, and my teeth were sharp. My canines punched into the soft meat of his throat easily. The copper tang of Jak's blood spilled into my mouth, a gush of red liquid.

It splattered onto the ground beneath us. He screamed, but the sound came out like a burble, and a rush of air. I had given him the chance to take a defeat once, and he had sprung a foul, deceitful attack on me.

That couldn't go unpunished.

I had to prove a point. I had to make sure that he never tried that again, not with anyone. Instincts overtook me.

I clenched my body, tightening my grip. His flesh gave even more between my canines. The punctures went deep, and the pain was enough to shock Jak out of his lynx shift and back into human form. His neck, still between my jaws.

The man screamed, and the sound sent blood spilling from the corners of his mouth, bubbling up in pink foam.

I dropped him, changing back into my human form. Looming over him, the gravity of what had just happened swept over me. His blood was in my mouth, but it had also soaked over the front of me. It ran in streaks down the curve of my neck, over my chin, and onto the ground.

My shirt was sodden with it. The stains would never come out. I would never forget the way that it tasted, either. Copper in my mouth. So much of it, that I could have drowned in the taste.

I had just killed a man.

This was bound to happen at some point. It was just how shifter society worked. People died. They were bound to die. I was bound to kill someone. Still, it knocked my legs out from under me and I crashed down onto my knees at Jak's side.

He was pale, the color gone from his face. Red was smeared all over his skin. One trembling hand shot up, grabbing onto the chain of my necklace – my mother's necklace. For a moment, I thought that it was Jak's last attempt to do something cruel. Then I realized that he was just trying to get me to lean closer.

I did.

It was like I was spellbound. There was no hesitation on my end. I bent down, so that our faces were only inches apart, and stared him straight in the eyes. One of my hands came down onto the ground beside his head, to keep me steady. The light was fading from his gaze. His pupils were pulled into narrowed slits, little dashes of black in a sea of murky faded color.

He opened his mouth. Blood and spit ran down his chin. Each rasping breath was harder for him to pull in than the last. On the exhales, more of his blood gushed from the punctures in his neck. Bruising had rapidly taken hold of him, mottling over the expanse of his throat. It was a transfer from when our fight had taken place in our shift forms.

I knew that my own body was showing similar marks, bruises, and scratches from where he had landed his blows. Several of the thinner lines on my arms began to knit together as I crouched there. None of his hits on me had been this bad, though.

I ached, but I would heal. The wound that I inflicted on Jak's neck, however, would never heal. It was too deep. I had hit him too hard. I had made one last move on him.

A literal last move.

"Why?" I demanded, my voice low and level, but still threatening. "Why would you do something like that?"

I needed to know. Why would he try and fight more,

even though I had already won? Was losing really that terrible of a thing? Had he just been trying to force my hand into revealing that I was the Prime Alpha?

If that was it, then why? How could it benefit him? And even more importantly, why had he tried to attack Oliver like that? Why was Petra so important to him?

If I didn't find out, then it would drive me absolutely mad.

His mouth moved a few times, tongue flicking against his teeth. For a moment, I thought that he wasn't going to be able to speak at all. That I had damaged his voice box and crushed his throat to a point where he could make no other sounds.

Then I realized that wasn't the case.

He was just... Struggling.

I waited.

The whole world seemed to be waiting with bated breath.

At least, it felt that way to me. Jak finally managed to find his voice, but it was so quiet that, even pressed this close to him, I could barely make out the words. It rattled and bubbled.

"The picture," Jak croaked, blood spilling forth with each syllable. He stopped, struggling to pull in enough air to keep talking. The sound was wet and obscene. A low whine came out on the exhale. Tears were spilling down the curve of Jak's face, over his cheeks. "Look in – Look... Look in the picture."

It seemed as though getting those few words out had drained him of what energy he'd been stubbornly clinging to. His body shivered, a full body motion, and his chest shuddered on an exhalation.

"The picture? What picture?" I demanded. I had no idea what he was talking about, but I knew that it was important.

It had to be.

Why else would he use his final moments to tell me about it? What else could be so important that he would choose to bring it up now?

Jak tried to say something else, but this time, the words wouldn't come. His hand slipped from where it had been clutched to my necklace, leaving behind nothing but a streak of ruddy, red blood. It fell onto the ground at his side.

"No!" The words came out a hiss. I grabbed at him, his shirt, his face. "No! You can't die without telling me what that's supposed to mean! Jak! Jakarta!"

"The picture," repeated Jak, but they were hardly even words. I wouldn't have been able to make them out if I didn't have advanced hearing.

"Jak," I hissed, my own voice dropping down low. "Jak, you need to tell me what that means. You need to tell me what that's supposed to mean!"

He trembled for a moment, and then let out a horrible rattling wheeze. Jak could no longer speak. The pool of red beneath us was truly massive. It stretched out, staining the ground, turning the once dusty earth into a muddy sort of mess.

I didn't press my hand to his neck. I didn't try to stop the flow of blood. I leaned backwards instead, staring down at Jak with wide eyes as the other shifter let out noisy, desperate, wet gasp. It was his last breath. Anyone could tell that.

His chest went still.

Jak was with us no more.

He was dead. And I was the one who had killed him.

22

They took me away from the corpse, but they didn't punish me.

I was pulled into the dining hall. Teachers hurried to usher students out, but they weren't all fast enough. Petra slipped in before they could get the big heavy doors shut. Her eyes were wide, her lips parted. She rushed to me, throwing her arms around my shoulders and pulling me in for a tight hug.

"I'm sorry," she gasped. "I'm sorry you had to do that!"

I wrapped my arms around her, protective warmth rushing through my veins. My chin pressed to her shoulder, and I breathed out in a harsh sort of chuffing sound. My nose pressed to the side of her neck, eyes slipping closed. I could still taste Jak's blood in the back of my mouth. Without the adrenaline of the fight rushing through me, it was harder to deal with.

"Are they going to expel me?" I asked her when she pulled back.

Petra shook her head. "For what?"

"Killing him." The words came out as a harsh croak. I had killed him. It hadn't quite sunken in yet.

"No," said Petra. "They won't. And you already know that. Come on, Victor. Come back to me. We've learned about the nuances before."

She was right. We had. It just felt different, having been the one to make that final bloody strike. This was no book we were reading from, no historical countenance or lecture in a classroom. It was real life. My fangs had ripped into Jak's throat, and I had felt his last breath shudder out over my own skin.

And my secret was out, too.

My body had taken on a new shape. It was impossible to deny that this could have been anything but my true ranking: Prime Alpha.

She ran her fingers over the side of my face, brushing against the corner of my eyes. She asked me, "Did you know?"

I gave a slight nod. "I wasn't allowed to tell anyone."

"Then... the old prime alpha?"

"Culled." The word came out bitter. I licked the blood from my teeth. My canines were still sharp as a lynx cat's. With the back of one hand, I wiped Jak's blood from my face. There was a ruckus at the doors. I took hold of Petra's hand and led her deeper into the dining hall, towards the back of it. Away from everyone else.

"This is going to change things," she said.

I flashed her the best attempt at a smile that I could muster. "We could have something."

"What?" Her eyes went wide.

My hands settled on her hips. I was desperate to find something good from this. I didn't regret killing Jak, but it had left me unsettled. I crowded Petra up against the wall of the dining hall, leaning down. Our mouths were close together, but I didn't kiss her. Not yet.

"We could have something," I said again. "Because I'm not just a bear kin shifter."

Her whole body seemed to flush as she realized what I meant. I held my breath, waiting to see – and then she gave the softest of nods, and an even softer smile. Her hand settled on my chest. "I would like that."

"You would?"

"I would."

That's when I kissed her. It wasn't as fierce as when we had crowded into the empty classroom, but it was passionate all the same. A part of me wondered if she could still taste the blood in my mouth. It wondered if she knew that I had killed Jak for her, above anything else.

From the look in her eyes when she pulled backwards, the answer to that was a solid, resounding yes. Petra let out a soft sigh. She leaned forward, letting her forehead rest on the curve of my shoulder. Her hands settled lightly on my sides.

"This is going to change a lot," she said, her voice whisper soft. "And I don't just mean for us. If you're Prime Alpha, they're going to expect certain things from you, Victor. They're going to want you to act a certain way."

I waited for her to straighten up some and then caught her chin, so that she had to look up at me. I told her, "I'm not going to act any way that I don't want. No one can make me do anything."

She looked uncertain for a moment, and then worried. Her teeth caught at her lower lip.

I insisted, "What?"

"It's going to be a lot more dangerous for you, too," said Petra, the worry clear in her voice.

She was concerned for me.

It was sweet, and I appreciated it but – it wasn't needed. I knew that they would come for me, just like they came for my father. And I wasn't going to let them get me.

"I'll be okay. I promise." I told her.

One of the teachers was heading towards me, Professor Blue. There was something like pride shining in his eyes. I wondered if it was for me, or for Monty.

Either way, it was my cue to pull away from Petra. I walked over to him, trying to remember to keep my shoulders pressed back and my chin lifted up. When I got close enough, he gave me a clap on the shoulder.

"You don't like listening to plans, do you?" Professor Blue asked.

I told him, "I wasn't planning on doing that. It just happened."

"It's a sign of strength, to have found your second shift so fast," said Professor Blue. "Your father was four years older than you before he could take on two forms."

"Really?"

Professor Blue nodded. "There will be questions. Things that you're going to need to deal with. We'll need to talk to you."

"About the fight?" I questioned.

But he shook his head. "About your class. Your role as Prime Alpha. But not tonight. Tonight, it's late, and we have to handle a bigger mess."

My gaze shifted to the door behind him. On the other side of it, I knew, lay Jak's body. "Someone's going to have to tell his parents."

Professor Blue stated, "It was a risk that he accepted when he came out and challenged you. Infighting happens. And his was done without honor."

"What happens to his family name?"

"That's not something you should worry about." Professor Blue kept his hand to my shoulder and steered me down the hallway, towards the door that led back outside. "What you need to do tonight is go back to your room and wait there for someone to come and get you in the morning."

That caught me by surprise. "What about my classes?"

"Someone will come and get you in the morning," insisted Professor Blue. "There are things to be handled that are more important than your classes."

It was a pretty daunting thing to say, but I could tell that the professor was serious. I nodded, shooting Petra one last look – and what I hoped was a reassuring smile – before turning and stepping outside.

The night smelled like blood, but Jak had already been removed from the school grounds. Several members of staff were out trying to clear away the mess. I wondered if they would erect something there for him. The teachers had been very brief in what happened when an alpha lost a fight, when it resulted in their death.

Was there any honor in it?

My first thought was that Jak didn't deserve that, any honor attached to his name. But then I thought about how far the Reed family had fallen, and what he had said right before he died. To look in the picture. It was like he had been trying to give me some kind of a warning.

And even before coming out there, I had come to the conclusion that Jak wasn't working alone. Someone else had been involved, pushing him forward, urging him to focus on me.

Had they told him to pick a fight with me?

Had they told him to hound after Petra?

I had too few answers. It was late. My head was spinning. My healing rate was faster than most other shifters, due to my status as prime alpha. The bulk of my injuries had already healed up, but I still felt drained.

Deciding that Professor Blue was right, I headed towards the building that contained the hall of alpha rooms. I had almost made it there when someone ran up behind me and grabbed me by the shoulder. I spun around snarling and snapping my fangs.

Reese Green pulled backwards, hands shooting up into the air between us. He gave a low keening whine and ducked his head, like he was trying to make his whole body seem smaller. It was a sign of submission if I had ever seen one, but I wasn't sure that I wanted to trust him just yet.

Still on guard, I demanded to know, "What?"

He shook his head at me. "Sorry. Didn't mean to startle you. I just wanted to come and congratulate you."

That surprised me.

I knew that he was one of Jak's closer allies. Lackey, more honestly.

Frowning, I asked, "Why?"

Reese ducked his head. "I just... wanted to."

For a moment, we both stood there in silence while I worked this out. I supposed that at heart, it was simply because I was the prime alpha, and that was what normal alphas were supposed to do. And it was what betas were supposed to do, too.

So, I gave a little nod, and I told him, "Thank you."

The relief that swept through his body was palpable. He

visibly relaxed and straightened up. Reese wasn't a bad looking guy but the grin that he gave me was nothing shy of goofy. Maybe the night had just been too long for him to try and act cool and put together.

"You were something out there," said Reese.

"Jak held his own." It was the most that I would give the man. My words were sharp and short, and seemed to get across the point that I wanted. I wasn't looking to stand and talk right now.

Reese instantly backed down, giving a little bit of a nod. "Right, well. That was it. I just wanted to make sure that I caught you and told you that. You know, congrats."

He turned and scurried off into the darkness, not quite with a tail between his legs but close to that. It was probably his attempt at showing me that I was where his loyalties rested now, but I wasn't certain that I was willing to accept them, not just yet. I had other things that needed to be gone over.

It wouldn't be smart to just take everything that was handed to me at face value. Considering the fact that Jak had to have been working with someone else, I had to be leery. There was no telling just yet how far the corruption ran, or how deeply connected the rest of his companions might have been.

I would tell Reese that I trusted him, but only so I could watch him. I would keep my enemies close until I was able to prove them my friend. That counted for Reese, and it counted for anyone else that tried to approach me in the coming days, now that they knew I was the prime alpha.

I imagined a lot of them would be looking for favors in the coming days, and I would need to be smart about which ones I gave out.

With that decision made up, I turned and stepped into

the building, heading towards the hall of rooms that the alphas had been given. No one else was inside, the commotion of our fight and Jak's death having drawn most of them outside. At least that meant for the time being, no one was going to come bother me.

23

My goal really was to just come up here and go to my room, get some rest before the absolute shit show that tomorrow was no doubt going to be. But then I caught sight of the door to Jak's room. Stepping over to it, I tested the handle.

Open.

A quick glance around proved that I was alone. I couldn't smell anyone coming up into the hallway either, even when I parted my mouth and let my shifter senses take over. With a deep breath, I pushed the door open and stepped inside. The door clicked shut behind me. I locked it, just in case anyone else tried to come nosing around.

The room looked pretty similar to mine, but somehow darker. Maybe that was just because I knew that the person who had been living here would never be coming back. Might've been it.

Everything smelled like Jak. There were a few pieces of laundry thrown over the foot of the bed. His workbooks were spread out over the desk, which was next to the window. I walked over and slid the window open, trying to make sure I could hear if anyone came up.

Nothing.

The night was silent.

With my mouth pulled into a thin line, I started looking through his room for anything that might have explained things. The last thing that Jak had said to me was *in the picture*. But it didn't look as though there were any pictures in his room. A painting hung above the bed, but that wasn't the same thing. Right?

Right.

Honestly, I had been expecting there to be some sort of a personal picture on the bedside table, or something like that sitting around in plain view. A picture that might have had a note tucked behind it, or that might have been taken of some kind of important meeting place.

But there wasn't anything.

I opened every drawer. Flipped through every book. Checked the insides of every bag, and even the pockets of the slacks. Maybe the picture just wasn't kept in plain view? Maybe it was something that he knew would give him away, so he kept it out of sight?

My searching grew more frantic. *In the picture*. That was the only hint that I had towards whatever this might have been. I had to be able to find one! I lifted up the mattress, checking to see if it had been shoved under there.

But – nothing.

There was nothing.

No hints. No clues. No explanations.

Frustration was building up inside of my chest. I let out an irritated growl, and paced through the room, raking my hands through my hair. What was I supposed to do now? This had been my only hope of figuring things out.

I was just about to storm out of the room in a fit of frus-

tration when my eyes landed on the painting that was
hanging on the wall above his bed.

There were no pictures in the room. No photographs, at
least. I had checked everywhere for one. So – the painting
must have been the picture in question. It seemed nonsen-
sical to me, but I didn't have any other explanations for what
Jak might have been talking about.

This was my last chance to figure it out. It took climbing
on the bed until I could reach it.

The mattress gave beneath my weight. It was like
walking on water.

Carefully, I took the painting off of the wall and laid it on
the mattress next to my feet. There was a cabinet hidden
behind it. The door was flat. I had to work it open using the
long tips of my claws. It came with a low creak, which had
my hair standing on end.

I froze, cocking my head to the side, but no one was
coming.

The door came open the rest of the way. There was a
simple wooden box inside. I pulled it to the edge of the
hidden cabinet and popped it open. Inside was a series of
letters, each one still in the envelope, with only the letter J
on the front.

No signage.

Nothing to go off of.

I didn't recognize the smell on the paper. They had all
been opened up already.

One of them read...

Jakarta

You haven't been keeping to your end of the deal. I thought

that you wanted things to get better? That you wanted the Reed name to have weight to it again? This isn't the way to do it. You must follow through with your end of the deal, or you'll get nothing.

You'll be nothing.

I'll make sure of it.

That was a threat if I had ever seen one. I knew that it wasn't just him. That would have been too impossible. I started to read through the other letters, hoping to figure out who might have been sending them.

I expect to see you after class. You're slacking. If you don't do better, I'll find someone else. There are plenty of other alphas looking to make something for their namesake out there. You were just the first. You don't need to be the last.

That letter made it seem like it was a teacher, someone that actively worked in the school. That made sense. I knew that some members of the staff were already aware that I was the prime alpha. That meant they might have let it slip to other people – or else, it meant that they might have already had a hand in the culling of my father.

Another letter.

We need someone beautiful. Did you really forget what the
woman was for? She's not yours. She never was.

And that one, it could only have been talking about Petra.
Alright, that was something to work off of. Whoever had
been writing to Jak, they had originally wanted to use Petra
for something. Blackmail against me, maybe, or something
to do with family lines.

Either way, I imagined that Jak had actually fallen for
her, and had been trying to find a way out of the deal.
Maybe he thought that if he killed me and just got me out of
the way, he wouldn't have had to keep working with
whoever had been sending the letters. It was clear that there
was something else going on.

Still one or two more layers to the secret, things that I
hadn't quite figured out.

But I would get there.

I always managed to get there in the end.

I was going to look through even more of the letters, but
I could hear footsteps approaching, and the sound of
someone trying the door handle. A voice, one of the
teacher's, muffled through the closed oak wood door.

Not wanting to get caught, I quickly shoved the letters
back into the box and closed the cabinet. The painting went
back up on the wall. The lock clicked open. I would never be
able to get out of there in time!

Panic shot through me, and I let my instincts take over.
My muscles bulged and my body twisted. The next thing
that I knew, I was on the ground, next to the bed, in my lynx
form.

Though I had only been in this form once before, it

still felt familiar, like a second skin. Something that I was meant to have. I continued to let myself be guided by my instincts, trusting them to be right. Pressing myself against the wall, I used the special ability that all lynx shifters had.

Shadow Sync rippled through my form, letting me fade into the shadows. The door swung open, but I was effectively gone from sight. That didn't mean no one could smell me if they were paying attention though, so I didn't linger for long. I made my way over to the window, grateful that I had opened it then.

The fresh air coming in from outside would help cover up my scent. I pulled myself out of it, dropping onto the balcony down below with a thump. I twisted, stepping into the shadows once more.

Someone came to the widow, a female voice. "It's a shame about what happened. We're going to have to try and get this room cleaned out fast, too. I don't understand why we have to rush it."

Another voice, a man's, "Because I said so." A pause. "And the headmaster agreed with me. The best thing that we can do right now is get this wrapped up fast. Think about the rumors that are going to start spreading."

"Rumors?" The woman laughed. "I saw that fight. They aren't rumors. That was him."

They were talking about me.

And Jak.

A note of sorrow swept over me. They were rushing through their job, then, because I was the prime alpha and my reputation had to be protected. Especially now, when I didn't have all of my shifts unlocked. The shadows were cool where they pressed against me, my black fur blending in with them seamlessly.

The fact that it was night out helped. The pitch black of the balcony was a good source of protection.

My ears pricked forward, craning to listen.

The woman was saying, "Bear kin to start with. And then lynx. You know what that means, don't you?"

The man snapped, "It means that you're not helping me get this done. Just close the window and let's get on with it."

The woman sighed. The sound carried down to me on the wind. There was a hiss and a shudder, and then the window closed. I gave a sigh of relief, stepping out of the shadows. For the first time, I looked through the sliding glass door of the balcony that I had landed on.

Cass was staring back at me.

I froze, and then I turned, and I jumped over the ridge of the balcony, landing neatly on the ground beneath. I didn't pause, sprinting towards the far side of the courtyard the moment that my paws were back under me.

Cass?

What the hell was she doing on this side of the building? The women didn't share the same dorm as us. It was a form of protection during rutting season, added walls and ground between us, so it was harder to scent them out. And I thought that it was also their attempt to keep up with the times and insist that the men here didn't run wild like they might have in the past.

Either way, she shouldn't have been in that room.

My mind was spinning.

Had someone already claimed her? Is that why she was there?

Better yet, why did I care?

I wasn't certain what the answer to that was. Only that I hated the thought of another man being all over her. It was just night. It was too late, and I had done too much.

The temptation to go back to my dorm was strong, but... I didn't want to run into the teachers on their way out of Jak's room, and I didn't want to run into any of the other students that were milling about on the grounds.

Those notes were from one of the professors here. That meant I had to be even more careful about who I trusted. Tonight, my emotions were already running wild. I couldn't go off there and risk making a decision that I would come to regret.

I had to keep my head on straight. I had to...

My gaze landed on the forest that surrounded the campus. My lynx form seemed to be drawn towards it; the trees and the shadows, and the scent of something wild carried to me on the cool night air.

What I needed, I realized, was to just get out of my own head for a little bit.

And what better way to do that than a night run?

With my mind made up, I took off into the tree line and deeper into the forest. My lean legs bunched and flexed with each springing step. This was vastly different than taking a run through the trees in my bear kin form. My gaze was at a different level, my ears keyed in on different things.

But the sensation was the same. The vigor that it sent through me. The deep connection with the world around me. And the way that it made my whole body seem to slide into a state of relaxation, acceptance, and understanding.

Each step took me further away from the academy and deeper into the darkness of the woods. The trees whipped at my hide and the dried leaves crunched beneath my paws. My eyes closed for a moment, head tilting up as I ran, letting the wind rush through the shaggy pelt of my lynx form.

I would go back to the Academy. I would figure out who

was blackmailing Jak and what they wanted with Petra –
what they wanted with me.

    But I wouldn't do it until the morning.

    I couldn't.

    For just a little while, I needed to run here and be free.

24

Early morning found me back in the room that they had given me. I climbed in through the window after my run through the woods, unwilling to go through the halls and run into someone else. It was the longest that I had stayed in a shifted form so far, and my body felt strange now, as though the human form was not where I truly belonged.

I had barely cleaned up when there was a knock on the door. Grumbling, I went to open it, honestly expecting to find that it was one of the teachers there, someone that had come to gather me for the supposed talk that I would need to have with the professors today.

It wasn't.

Monty stared at me.

He had a strange expression on his face, not quite cowed but close to that. "Hey. Can I come in?"

"Sure." I stepped aside, letting Monty in. Then I peeked out the door, glancing up and down the halls. No one. The door to Jak's room was closed. I imagined that it was probably locked, too.

Stepping back into my own room, and closing the door with a soft click, I turned to face Monty. "What's going on?"

"Is it really a hard guess?"

"I mean, I know that you're here about last night. If it's to hassle me about something, you might want to get in line." I snorted, pulling out the chair by my desk and dropping down into it. "The professors have first dibs on that."

Monty asked, "You're really the prime then?"

I nod. "Sorry. I wasn't supposed to tell anyone."

Monty laughed. "You did a bad job at that. I think more people are talking about you than they are talking about Jak."

That made me feel... Odd.

Jak was an asshole. But did his death deserve to be dismissed? I wasn't certain. This was a society that I had barely been part of. I would have to try and see how everyone else reacted, once the acclaim over my true ranking came out.

"It was an accident," I admitted. "I've never changed into a lynx before."

"So that was your first dual shift?"

"Is that what it's called?"

Monty shrugged. "That's what my dad called it. You know, because you have two forms to change between."

I nodded. "Makes sense. And yeah, it was. I've never done anything like that before. When he jumped me..."

Monty shook his head, a look of disgust crossing his face. "That was a coward's move."

"I don't think it was that. I think it was desperation." If there was one person I could trust, it would be Monty. "I don't have proof of it. Not on me. I put it back. He was working with someone. For someone, I think."

"How do you know that?".

"I went into Jak's room last night."

"What? Why would you do that?"

"Before he died-" Before I killed him, when his blood still dripped from my mouth. Before I felt his last breath shudder out against my skin. "He told me that I needed to look behind the picture. So, I did. There's a painting in his room, above his bed."

"They cleared the room out last night. I don't know why. One of the teachers said that it needed to be fast tracked."

"It's a good thing that I'm faster than they are," I said, with a shake of my head. "There was a box behind the painting, filled with letters." In hindsight, I should have known someone like Jak wouldn't have been that semantic about things. I should have looked behind the painting, first. "Someone was blackmailing Jak. I don't know why, and I don't – I don't know all of the details. But they wanted Petra, and I'm positive that it was someone on the staff."

I had thought about taking the letters with me. But I wanted to make sure that whoever had been blackmailing Jak didn't know I was gathering information on them. In the grand scheme of things, Jak was a small fry. I needed to catch the one that was *blackmailing* him. That was the important thing.

Monty's eyes went wide. "A professor?"

I nodded, my mouth pulled into a serious grimace. "I know that it's someone on staff."

"If they're on staff, it's good that you didn't take the letters," said Monty. "Not until we know which professor it is. If they were on the crew that cleared his room out, they would have seen the missing letters and gotten rid of any other evidence that could lead us towards them."

"That's what I was thinking, too." I nodded. "They must

have known who I was. And... I don't know. I don't know why they would have wanted Petra."

Anger and protective instinct surged up at the thought. She had already been chased so much by Jak. It wasn't fair that someone was still after her, especially when I didn't know what they might have been looking for.

It couldn't JUST be that I was interested in her, right?

Even with my status as a prime alpha, that just seemed... Like it wouldn't be enough.

"I don't know what they're looking for, or what their goal is. But I'm going to find out, Monty," I told him. "They're going to regret ever messing with me, or with Petra."

No hesitation. Monty stepped towards me, placing a hand on the desk. "I want to help."

"What?"

"That's what I came up here for, Victor," said Monty. "I want to help. And not just with figuring out who was twisting Jak's arm, or what they want with Petra. If you're the prime alpha, then I want to help protect you, through everything."

It felt like the very air in the room seemed to change, a sharp stutter of electricity that bounced through it. I sat up straighter, almost without thinking about it. An instinctual stiffening of the spine, and a straightening of the shoulders.

"Why?" I asked.

"Because you're – you're the prime. And you're going to be a good one, I can tell," said Monty. "My father, he was a general for the last prime. And he told me what it was like; told me what to expect. I can help you figure this out, Victor. Let me be your general."

The professors had spent very, very little time talking about primes and generals. It wasn't meant to be on the syllabus until the next semester, after we had all gone through our first rut. Something to help wrap things up, once we had cemented who was the head alpha of each phenotype.

But... If I was a prime, then I couldn't be the head of the bear kin. Those were two different roles. And that meant that Monty was the next strongest.

Head of the bear kin, and a good man, to boot.

He had jumped into that fight yesterday without a second thought. And he had his own loyal following. If Monty was sworn into my loyalty, then his beta pack would follow along, too. I would have a good following, and my announcement as prime wouldn't even be public yet.

I nodded, just once.

Best to let Monty take the lead here, since he seemed to know more about it than I did.

The man took a knee in front of me. I stood up without thinking, so that I towered above him. His head bowed in submission, and his eyes settled on my feet. This was more than just an agreement of words. I could feel that shift in the air again, only now, it was gathering around me, condensing around me.

It crackled over my skin and pushed into my veins. My mouth was watering.

"I swear to fulfill, to the best of my ability and judgment, this covenant: I will bear true faith and allegiance to the prime alpha, Victor; I will give to him my blood and my breath, and spill both onto the earth should that toil be requested. At his side, in his graces, I will command those given to me for protection, and I will provide the same to my alpha prime, in whatever manner is requested." Monty said.

The words seemed to echo around the room, as though they were being spoken by a thousand other people. I could smell them, too, every other man and woman that had taken this oath. They had come here, in spiritual presence, their ancestral forms clinging to this oath of loyalty.

It was not one that could easily be broken.

Though I did not really know the words, I responded in due turn, letting my own ancestors guide my tongue.

I told him, "You who have sworn to me, blood and breath, death and life; you have given to me what few others would give. In your hands, I place the bear kin and my back."

The world seemed to shudder, a breath of exhaled relief at the response. I could feel it, a new power in me. Monty's strength had become mine. I didn't know what he felt. All I knew was that his eyes had slipped shut and a look of pure contentment had settled on his features.

Slowly, he stood up. When he did, I clasped hold of his hand with one hand, and his elbow with the other, and he returned the gesture. Our eyes met. I knew that this was a man who would die to defend me.

Did my father have men like that? He must have. Professor Blue was his general, and I could not see Monty's father ever betraying anyone, the same way that I could not see Monty ever betraying me. I knew that he would be at my side, until the very end.

With any luck, that would not be for a long time.

When the grip was broken, the sensation in the other vanished. The sacred oath had been made. I knew that I could trust him.

Monty cleared his throat, trying to pull himself back together. "What happens next?"

"I'm not sure. I need to speak with the professors. They want me to come to some big meeting, to discuss the fact that I'm the prime. My uncle only told a few people when I arrived. He didn't want me to be in any undue danger," I explained. "Especially since I wasn't raised in a shifter family."

Monty nodded. "That makes sense, but it's not helpful now. Everyone knows who you are."

"I think that must be what the meeting is about. Are they... Going to let me finish taking classes?"

"You mean before they start expecting you to lead?"

I nodded.

Monty thought about it for a moment. Then he said, "I don't think that they have a choice, if that's what you want. Victor, they aren't in charge of you." A pause. "You're in charge of them."

The realization seemed to wash over me out of nowhere. Monty was right. The tides had changed. I might have been a student here, but I wasn't some first cut alpha. I was the prime. And even the senior alphas on the staff would need to listen to what I had to say, if I made it clear that it was an order.

That was a lot of power. It was almost heady, realizing that it was all mine to control.

I didn't let my thoughts linger on that for long, though. It wouldn't be the least bit helpful to be prideful. I needed, instead, to make sure that I was smart about this. That would be what truly made me stand out as a prime alpha.

"I want you to find Petra," I said. "I don't have the time between now and when I have to leave. But I need to make sure that she's alright."

"I can do that." Monty barely waited to make sure that it was my only request before turning and rushing from the room, seemingly eager to have received his first order as my general. I knew that, over time, there would be other generals to stand at my side. But I couldn't help but think that none of them would be as good as Monty.

He would be my first.

He would be my best.

And when time came for a battle, he would be the last one standing, too.

I could trust him to keep Petra safe, even if there was no one else in the Academy that held my trust.

25

The first knock hit the door, and I figured that it was one of the teachers that was coming to get me. You know, since Monty had already left. But then I stepped closer to the door, and I caught a whiff of vanilla and peaches. A smile curled over my face as I pulled open the door, and then pulled Petra into my arms. They wrapped around her, and she burrowed against me.

"I'm glad you're okay," Petra said. "I know what happened. And I was worried."

"You didn't need to be worried." I pulled her more fully into the room, away from the door. It clicked shut behind us. Before she could say anything else, I plastered my mouth against hers, catching her in a kiss.

Petra deepened it, her hands curling in the front of my shirt. Our tongues pressed together, and the smell of her flooded me, filling me from the inside out. Peach pie, and the taste of Petra on my tongue. I nipped at her lower lip and pushed her backwards against the wall.

"You took care of him," said Petra, her voice soft and wavering. "You took care of him for me."

"I told you that I would." My hands shoved up under the hem of her shirt. Nails scraped lightly over the curve of her ribs. I did my best to memorize the shape of her body, to take in everything about her.

She kissed me again, tangling a hand in my hair and giving the slightest of tugs. I wanted to lose myself in her. I wanted her to be here with me, to never leave.

To be mine.

She let out a sound, a soft keening little whine, and pressed a hand up under my shirt, too, running her fingers over my bare skin, and feeling the softness of my belly. She said, "I think that... I think that I might want to."

I didn't need to ask her what she was talking about. "Are you sure?" I thought about what Professor Balboa had told us about how marriage and claimings between shifters had changed over the last few decades. There had been a time when it was used to help influence politics. Omega children were offered to alphas in high political positions, the same way that Victorian fathers would offer their daughters to Lords who could pay high dowries. "I don't want to do this just because you think that you need to thank me."

"I don't feel that way," said Petra. "And it's sweet that you're so concerned. I'm okay. I promise. I want this." She kissed me again. "I want you."

My hands dropped to her hips. I backed her over to the bed and pushed her down onto it. Petra spread her legs, so there was room for me to stand. She sat on the edge of the mattress, and I leaned down to keep kissing her, only parting when I pulled the shirt free from her body.

Her bra was pale pink and lace. It fit her in ways that I couldn't quite grasp. The texture of it, the way that it pressed to her tits. I ran my hand over her left breast and gave it a squeeze. Then I reached around, my fingers about to curl around the clasp of her bra when-

Knock, knock, knock.

The sound startled me. I snarled at the door. "What the hell is wrong with everything this morning?"

Petra let out a laugh and said,, "Hand me my shirt before you open the door."

"I don't want you to put your shirt back on," I protested, leaning to kiss her. The underside of her jaw, the side of her neck. My hands ran over her arms, and then finally pulled away, when the knocking got even louder and more persistent.

Petra slipped out from under my arms, and she grabbed her shirt. She reached up, paused, and then unhooked the back clasp of her bra. She let the lacy pink fabric fall away, and I was given my first real look at her tits, perky, pretty things with dusky nipples.

Then the shirt was pulled on. Before she could pick the bra back up, I bent down and grabbed it. "I'll keep this."

It was meant to be a playful joke, something to lighten the mood and make sure that she stayed comfortable. And hey, maybe I would have use for it later. Whoever was twisting Jak's arm had wanted Petra for something. Having a piece of clothing that smelled as strongly of peach pie as this bra did might help.

Petra laughed again, leaning forward to kiss me. "Consider it a thank you for all of the help that you gave me."

"You don't need to thank me," I told her. "I'll do anything and everything to protect you. No matter who it's up against."

I pulled her in for one last kiss, the slide of our lips slick and soft and achingly tender. I could have lost myself in it, the taste of her, the smell of her, the way that she wrapped around me. Her arms slipped around my shoulders and then ran down, pushing me slightly away from me.

And then she turned and went to the door, pulling it open herself. "Hi, Professor Blue."

"Petra." Professor Blue sounded more amused than anything at the sight of her. I'm sure that he could smell her through the door.

"Good luck today," said Petra, and then she turned, and she made her way down the hall, vanishing from sight. The woman had an ass like nothing else. I couldn't help but lean forward, craning my head to the side to watch her go.

When she was gone from my sight, I straightened up and I gave Professor Blue a smile. "Let me guess. You're here to take me to the meeting?"

"Something like that," said the professor. He gestured at me, waiting for me to finish getting dressed. Only then did he let me out of the room, and into the hallway. I felt odd next to the man. He had so much more experience than I did, but was somehow beneath me in the pecking order. That would take some serious getting used to.

We took a few steps, and then he stopped me. "I know that we have to be quick, but I need to give you something."

"Alright?" I frowned. "Is everything okay?"

"I worked very closely with your father," said Professor Blue. "And I know that you're going to need to be more careful than he ever was."

Because he had been culled. And whoever did it, they would try to cull me, too.

"This is for you." From his jacket, he pulled out a letter. It had a red wax seal on it, but the seal was faded, like it had been stamped into place a long time ago.

"What is this?" I took it, running my finger over the circle of wax. The seal was strange, a deer's head, with something around it, bells or flowers, a ring around the head, between the antlers.

"When you're out of the meeting, find somewhere to open that. Make sure you're alone when you do it," said Professor Blue.

"What is it though?"

"Just do what I'm saying."

I tucked the envelope back into my jacket pocket on the inside, and then I nodded at him. "Alright. Are you able to give me some kind of a heads up? Like, is it bad news at least?"

The professor chuckled and started walking again, leading me further down the hallway and through the buildings. I went with him, at least partially because I didn't have a say in it. "When we get there, you're going to need to try and watch what you say."

"How so?"

"I know that it can be tempting for a new prime alpha to try and throw their weight around," said Professor Blue. He still looked like he could barely fit into the jacket and the white dress shirt. I thought that he would have been better if he just wore leathers and armor all the time.

It would have been a more fitting look at least, especially with the scars.

He had been a good general for my father. I'm sure that his son would be a good general for me, too. I wondered, did Professor Blue already know that his son had taken the sacred oath? Did he know that I had gained a general already?

If he did, it wasn't mentioned. Instead, the walk to the meeting was filled with Professor Blue telling me about the different teachers, who he thought I might be able to get on my side, and what to expect out of it. How they just wanted to know how far into my prime state I had gotten, and if I knew what had happened to my father.

That sort of thing.

No mention of Jakarta's death was made.

I couldn't figure out why that bothered me so much.

26

They gathered me about five minutes after Petra left and took me into a room that I had never been in before. It could only have been a teacher's lounge or meant specifically for meetings among the staff. Everyone was there, even the professors whose class I had attended only once or twice, and those who taught electives that I hadn't signed up for.

They sat me at the head of the table, and then... we waited.

Over half an hour later and my patience had worn thin.

Irritation was starting to curl in me. "You brought me out here, and won't even speak?"

"Professor Beaumont isn't here yet," said Professor Blue. There was a tightness to his words. "I think it's best if we wait for him."

My lips pulled into a thin line. It was a struggle, finding the balance between being in charge and not just being a raging asshole. I waited three more minutes and then cleared my throat.

"Enough. I'm not going to sit here any longer. You're either going to talk to me, or I'll leave," I told them.

Professor Balboa said, "He's right. We can't let this drag out forever. We need to talk. Why did no one inform me that the prime alpha was a student here?"

"Aaron thought it best if that information about his nephew was kept on the need to know," said Professor Blue.

Professor Balboa narrowed his eyes. "Of course, you would need to know." And then, more loudly, "Does this mean that Adrian is dead?"

"Of course, it does," said Professor Beaumont, finally stepping into the room. "Adrian Rawlings is just as dead as poor Mister Jakarta."

I held my ground, tilting my head back. "The fight was over, and he attacked from behind. That makes it legal, within our standings."

And even if it wasn't, no one would challenge me.

Aaron, he said that my father was smart but that he was mean. He had been making headway bringing in power from other houses, but he didn't have many fans. I wanted a different legacy.

The prime alpha that fixed the houses.

The one who wasn't culled.

"He's right," said Professor Blue. "My son was involved in the fights. I've already heard what happened."

"I would never question the legitimacy of it," said Professor Beaumont. "I just think it should be noted that the fight took place on Academy grounds."

Professor Balboa asked, "What does that have to do with anything?"

"We've never had a prime alpha this young before," said Professor Beaumont.

"My age doesn't factor into anything," I responded, firmly.

Professor Beaumont hummed. He took his seat, gesturing for the conversation from earlier to continue.

After a moment of stumbling, Professor Balboa asked, "What does this mean for us?"

Professor Blue said, "He was working on forming alliances with the other houses when he was culled."

A muttering broke through the table. Not sickness then. Culled. Murdered. Whatever my mother had been running from when she took me and left him, it had caught up to my father in the end.

I had never known the man and could not mourn him. My mother had made sure of that. She didn't want me to have anything to do with him. Now, I knew it was because she was trying to keep me away from this society. She knew that being involved in the Apex Academy would put me in danger.

At the time, though, when I was younger, I thought that it was because he'd been an awful guy. But it was clear that many of these professors had been dear friends with my father. They mourned, and they grieved, and Professor Blue, the general, my father's right-hand man, sat there in silence as they did.

But the silence didn't last long.

A shrill alarm suddenly split through the air. My head snapped up, hands flying to press against my ears. "Ugh! What is that?"

"Fire alarm," Professor Emily Hart said. She jerked up onto her feet, her eyes went wide. She taught alchemy and herbalism, though I wasn't taking either class. She hurried over to the window, slamming it open.

The bitter tang of smoke flooded the room.

Professor Balboa was already on his feet and lurching

out of the room. Professor Blue stood up as well, the legs of his chair scraping over the tile floor. "Where at?"

"It's on the other side of the campus," said Professor Hart.

Other teachers were rushing outside now, each one desperate not only to see what was happening and make sure that the students were alright, but to make sure that it didn't spread. Firemen would not come to our Academy, after all. It was a hidden location, away from the rest of the world.

To bring people out here – even for an emergency – it just could never happen. We would need to handle the problem ourselves. That meant that for the time being, the meeting was canceled, and the discussion of my role was over with.

It seemed too convenient to be true, but I followed the professors as they made their way to the door. Before I could step out into the hallway, Professor Beaumont reached out and put a hand on my shoulder. "I would be very careful, Victor."

I shrugged out from under his grip. "What?"

"It can be easy to mistake who is on your side and who isn't," said the professor. His gazer flicked to the hallway. At first, I thought that he must have known that it was someone in my father's own court that betrayed him.

But then I realized that it was more than that.

He wasn't concerned with my father's death. He just wanted me to back him, and his decisions. A pitiful vie for power, long before it was acceptable to make one.

"I can figure out who is going to be good for my pack just fine," I said, tartly.

Professor Beaumont shook his head. "Your father thought the same thing and look where it got him. You need someone more worldly to help. I can do that. I can tell you all there is to know about the Elder Alphas and Elder Betas in your command."

It was a tempting offer, but only for a moment. I didn't like the look in Professor Beaumont's eyes. I didn't like the sharp, upward curl of his smile. The way that he was looking at me, as if I was nothing more than a piece of meat?

"I can shape my own bonds," I told him, firmly. I wanted to make some sort of a big dramatic exit to really push that in, but the man's head suddenly snapped to the side, towards the hallway.

A different smile crossed his face. He stepped out into the hallway, and over to a woman that was standing there.

She was a lion shifter, which I thought was unusual. I had never seen one like her before, a female lioness. And she stood there with such a demure bob to her head, this little curl down of the shoulders.

I didn't like it.

The woman stepped over to Professor Beaumont, meeting him halfway. She reached out, and he curled an arm around her waist, sweeping her up against his side. I didn't know why, but something about the way that she was moving and standing just rubbed me the wrong way.

Were there any lion shifters in the academy?

There weren't. And she didn't smell like any of the other shifters from our house, either. She didn't smell like anything, actually.

I was reminded of the cologne that my uncle had given me; a scent blocker, normally used to strip the tang of blood from our skin. There was no smoke on her. Nothing that told me who she had been speaking with recently. And no lingering traces of the other students or professors on her skin.

Was she… From somewhere else? What had she been using the scent blocker for?

They didn't linger in the hallway for long, going in the other direction. They didn't seem to be particularly concerned with the fire, either, but I was. The alarm was still going off. I turned and went the other way, towards the sound.

It was easy to find. The moment that I stepped outside, I could see the big, thick plume of black smoke that spilled up into the sky above. It was a towering thing, a pillar of black that came from the other side of the campus.

There were plenty of other people standing around, watching. I latched onto Monty and went over to him. "What's going on?"

"I don't know how it started, but the delta building got lit up," said Monty.

"The delta building? Were people inside?"

Monty shook his head. "No one's said much of anything yet, but I think that they've almost got the fire under control." He looked at me. "How did that meeting go?"

"It didn't. We had to wait for Professor Beaumont to show up. When he did, the alarm went off and we all left," I explained. "But… There was something. There was a lion shifter."

"Oh, that must have been Hannah."

"I thought that there were only the five phenotypes." I frowned, still thinking about the lack of smell on her.

"In our house, sure. But some other places have different animals. You know, you're not going to find anything cold blooded up in the northern hemisphere kind of thing," said Monty.

I supposed that made sense. I asked him, "What's… their deal? Are they mates?"

"Sort of. Beaumont claimed Hannah through an old guard method. He asked Hannah's father for permission, and the guy gave her away," said Monty.

"So, she didn't have a say in it?"

"No."

"How's that possible?" I asked. "I mean, how can you just-"

"It's like the Victorian times," said Monty. "You know, when people have a dowry. Or when they would give their daughters away for money. People don't do it anymore, not really. Only if you're an old school guy. We covered it in history class, remember?"

He was right. Professor Balboa had mentioned it. With everything going on, I was just too scattered to remember it.

I thought about it for a moment. I knew that Professor Beaumont was an old school guy. He was older, and he had a lot of old-style views on things. I knew that it would be like changing, I don't know, a preacher from the ninety's opinion on something.

There was a shout from the other side of the grounds. The building seemed to let out a spark of light. And then it exploded with a deafening sort of crack, and a blast of heat that swept out across the grounds. The scent of smoke was too much for most of the shifters.

A lot of the other students went back inside, to get away from it. Even my nose wrinkled up, my lip peeling back with distaste to show off my teeth.

Monty was in the same state as me. He suggested, "We should get inside. This is starting to give me a headache."

"Alright. I'll follow you." I said.

Monty stepped away and started towards the building. He only made it a few steps before he stopped, realizing that I wasn't following.

"I don't understand how something like that could have happened," I said, staring at the smoke. It was billowing even thicker now, a second plume of darkness spilled up into the sky. "I mean, someone had to have set it, right?"

"A fire like that?" Monty looked towards the smoke, too. His face was twisted up with distaste at the tang in the air, and the thought that someone could hold such scorn towards the deltas, they would do something like this.

We both stood there for a long moment, just staring up at the clouds that pulled above us. Then he finally shook his head.

"It's too convenient," said Monty. "That started right before your meeting could? I think someone set it on purpose."

I asked, "Do you think it could have been Hannah? When I saw her earlier, she didn't have any smoke on her."

"What?" Monty frowned, and then shook his head. "Why would it have been her?"

"Still working on that," I told him, hesitantly, as I was still piecing things together myself. "But she had scent blocker on her. She was trying to hide something. Maybe... Maybe she knew that the smoke would have been clinging more heavily to her than it was anyone else. She used the scent blocker to try and cover it."

Monty frowned. He didn't seem dismissive of the idea, he just looked thoughtful. "I don't actually know anything about her, just that they didn't claim each other in the modern way. She might have, but I don't see why."

"What if it was him?" I asked, the pieces starting to take shape into a greater picture. "What if the one that was pulling Jak's arm was Beaumont? And then he had Hannah show up and set the fire as a distraction?"

Monty thought about it for a moment. "I think it's worth

looking into. I'll see if anyone that I know might have heard why Hannah came by today, or where she was at before finding Beaumont. If she was loitering around near the delta house..."

"Then that's who we need to be careful around," I said, with a nod of my head. It wasn't a sure-fire answer. It wasn't even a sure-fire solution that this might be the answer. But I thought that having a direction to look in was better than not having anything at all.

I would keep an eye on Professor Beaumont... And we would figure something else out. Monty, Petra, and I.

We weren't alone.

We would get through this, together.

It was then that I remembered the letter that Professor Blue had given me. The one that was still in my jacket pocket. Once we were in the building, I told him, "Go find Petra. See if you guys can meet me in the library. There's something that I need to do first."

Monty nodded and left. I didn't want to just open the letter up in the middle of the halls, so I looked around, eventually finding an empty classroom to sit down in. I locked the door, just to make sure no one would come barging in.

I had learned my lesson. Enough people had shown up knocking during something important to last me a lifetime, let alone a single day.

Once I was certain that no one else was around, I pulled out the letter and rolled it between my hands a few times. There were no words written on it, not on the front of it or the back. The only indication that it was of personal value was the seal.

I stared at it, trying to wrack my brain about what the sigil might have meant. To my knowledge, there was no such thing as a deer shift – though I would admit, up until seeing Hannah, I had thought that there were no lion shifts, either.

Of course, it could just be a crest for someone's name and not have anything to do with the shift of the person. On closer inspection, the wreath around the stag's antlers was made of flowers that resembled bluebells.

I sniffed the paper but could only pick up Professor Blue on it. Either it was old, cleaned, or I just... I don't know. I had gotten pretty good about picking things up with my nose. Guess this was just the exception.

Taking a deep breath, I ran the tip of my sharpened nail through the thick seal of wax, splitting it open and letting the letter slide out. And then, alone in the room, I began to read.

27

We met at the base of one of the trees, just outside of the main grounds for the school. Monty and Petra were there waiting when I showed up. It felt like there was a heavy weight in the back of my chest, weighing me down. Each step forward kicked up more dust.

Monty frowned. "What happened?"

Petra got on her feet and hurried over to me. "I was worried that the fire might have had something to do with you."

"I think that it did." I gave her a hug, wrapping one arm around her waist, and then pressed a kiss to the side of her face, another on her mouth. It felt wrong to separate from her. We hadn't been able to officially claim each other yet, and that was biting at me like a mosquito that wouldn't leave.

I wanted her.

God, I wanted her.

But even my want was going to need to wait in the face of what I had just learned.

I pulled the letter from my pocket. Monty asked, "What is that?"

"Your dad gave it to me," I said, frowning. I stepped closer to the tree. The other two crowded in around me. "It's a letter. From my dad."

The silence weighed down on us all. They knew that I had never met my dad. And after the fight with Jak, they knew that he was dead, too.

The prime, gone.

My father, gone.

Gone, before I could even meet him.

My mouth was dry. I looked at the letter again, taking in the unfamiliar script. I had never seen it before, and yet there were similarities. We formed our B's the same way. We wrote in quick, tight cursive. His handwriting was a little on the shaky side compared to mine, but still.

Still.

My father wrote this letter.

Petra's hand settled on the small of my back. It was warm, even through the blazer that I was wearing. I rocked back into it, just a little, seeking comfort from the touch.

Victor,

By the time you get this, I will be dead. I have entrusted it to my general. Grant is a good man. If you trust no one else, you can trust him and his kin. I am sorry. There is much that I wish I could have told you. Could have done for you. I don't have the time to list it all. I doubt that you would want to see it. You know where I have failed. You and your mother both know.

Even reading the letter for the second time has my eyes burning again. At my side, Monty stood a little bit straighter. Praise from the last prime, even written, was something worth being proud of. I was certain that it had given him a boost.

I took a deep breath, trying to calm my nerves, and turned back to the letter.

But you cannot trust everyone. Victor, there is too much that has happened to write down. I don't have the time. Don't have the words for it. Someone has betrayed me. Someone that I trusted. They have let House Renoir in. They are coming for me. The wolves will be at my door any minute now. When they arrive, they'll cull me.

"House Renoir?" Petra shook her head. "That's terrifying."

"We knew that Mikel was on our grounds," said Monty.

Petra admitted, "I thought that it was just a rumor. Something that people were making up. Who would have invited him in?"

"Someone that the Dean trusted," said Monty.

"Or the Dean himself," I added. "We can't rule out anyone." A pause. "Except for your dad, I guess."

Monty beamed. He was a big guy, but there was a softness under his gruff facade. He had the kind of heart that thrived on praise.

I shook the letter, just a little bit. "Finish reading it."

His gaze snapped back to the piece of paper. The end of the letter had ink spots on it, scattered over the parchment. I wondered if my dad had been using a traditional pen, the kind that needed an ink well.

He will stop at nothing to take this house. And whoever is helping him, they will stop at nothing to *give* it to him. Be careful. Be smart. Be strong. Be lethal.

And then his name was signed at the bottom of the letter.

That was it.

The only time he had ever spoken to me, and that was it. The rage I felt the first time that I read through that letter rose up inside of me again. A low growl rumbled through my chest, but my friends wrote it off as being angry over the betrayal.

I was pissed about that, too. It was complicated. Complicated, and almost too much.

"So, someone here invited Mikel in. And they helped betray your dad," said Monty, frowning.

Petra was oddly quiet.

I folded the letter, making sure to use the existing creases, and tucked it back into the envelope. I slipped the envelope into my back pocket, so I could take it to my room.

Petra still said nothing.

"What's wrong?" I asked her, sensing the unease.

She shook her head. "Maybe it's nothing but... I don't think that it was the Dean."

Monty asked, "Why not?"

"You said that it was a professor twisting Jak's arm," Petra said, nodding at me.

"That's what the letters said," I explained. "They told Jak to stay behind after class let out."

"What?" Monty frowned. "You didn't say that before. I would have known where to look, if you had."

"There was a lot going on," I told him, frustrated. At the time, keeping myself out of the spotlight had seemed important.

Even Monty had agreed with me.

I was quick to remind him, "You didn't want me to take the letters either, remember? It would have been too big of a giveaway that we were onto someone on the staff."

Monty said, "And I stand by that. You shouldn't have taken the letters. But you should have told me that Jak was supposed to stay behind after class."

I snapped, "Why does it matter? It was a professor here; we knew that already."

Monty told me, "Because there's only one class that ever kept Jak back. Beaumont's."

Silence rang through.

"What?" I asked.

Monty nodded. "Yeah. He was always getting held back in Beaumont's class. You two never noticed?"

A shudder ran through Petra. She wrapped her arms around her chest, almost protectively. "I did my best to keep away from him. He was a slime bag."

"He was," I agreed. "You're sure that it was Beaumont's?"

Monty nodded. "Positive."

"That... Makes sense," I said. "When we had our meeting, he was late. And his mate, she was here. Remember I told you that?"

I caught Petra up on what had happened at the meeting, the way that Beaumont had been acting weird, and how strange it seemed that his mate had showed up at the Academy.

Monty said, "I think that they started the fire. It was a distraction for something."

"For letting Mikel onto the grounds again?" I offered. "We know that he was here once already. The fire would have been a good way to keep everyone's focus elsewhere."

Monty pointed out, "That's why Beaumont had Hannah do it."

Petra said, "No one would look twice to see her out here. She could have said that she was just visiting her mate. And with that scent blocker...."

"No one would have been able to tell that she was right there at the start of the fire. So, connecting it all." I paused, and then ran through the list myself, "Beaumont was twisting Jak's arm, and he wanted Petra for something. And his mate, she's our biggest suspect for having started that fire. In fact, it's practically a sure thing. Anyone else, it would have been smelled on them."

"We just need to figure out why they wanted Mikel back here," said Monty. "I think we split up today, talk to different people. See if anyone knows anything."

It was the best that we could come up with. Monty left first, leaving Petra and I alone. Though we didn't have much time before we would have to part ways too, we spent it with each other, sitting at the base of the tree. Petra stayed in my lap, my arms wrapped around her. I rested my chin on her shoulder, my lips pressed firmly to her neck.

All I could think about was biting her.

It was a ceremony. A claiming bite. Professor Balboa had taught us that. It was one of the stranger lessons that we had sat through.

Petra put a hand over my wrist. Her skin was soft. "Do you think... what do you think they wanted me for?"

"I don't know," I admitted. "But it doesn't matter. They aren't going to have you."

"Beaumont is older than you. Stronger."

"I'll kill him," I said. "If he touches you."

The words tasted strange. I didn't relish the thought of killing someone else. Having done that to Jak, it was hard on me. The taste of his blood still seemed to linger in the back of my mouth. But the thought of someone bringing harm to Petra, that was even worse. It made my skin crawl.

I knew that, if it came down to that, I really would kill Beaumont.

Eventually, we couldn't put off going and trying to do our research any longer. Petra uncurled from my lap, turning and pressing a lingering kiss to my lips. I took the chance to lick into her mouth, tasting her more fully, before she stood up and left.

For a while, I just sat there at the base of the tree, trying to think about everything that had happened, everything that I had learned.

I pulled the envelope out and looked at it again, though I didn't open it. I wondered what my father had been doing when he wrote this. How close to his death had it been penned? How long had Professor Blue been carrying it around?

That tightness came back to my chest, like fingers wrapped around me.

It wasn't fair.

I hated this man. I *hated* him. But I also wished that I knew more about him. I wanted to spit in his face just as badly as I wanted him to tell me in person that he was sorry.

Writing it down like this didn't mean anything, not really.

Frowning, I pulled myself to my feet. Sitting around

wasn't going to change anything. No amount of anger or irritation was going to be enough to bring him back. I wouldn't know what to say, even if it did. I tucked the envelope back into my pocket for safekeeping and headed back towards the main grounds of the Academy.

The smoke was still spilling up in great, thick plumes from where the delta house had been burned down. I found one of the other students, Cass, and asked her, "Have they said anything else about the fire yet?"

She gave me an odd look. I wondered if she was going to address the fact that I had revealed myself as prime the night before, but she just ended up shaking her head. It seemed that the fire had rattled everyone too. "You didn't hear?"

"Hear what?" I frowned.

Cass nodded towards the smoke. "They've canceled classes for the next two days. I guess that the fire wasn't an accident. Someone set it on purpose."

"Arson?" I tried to sound surprised, but that actually just confirmed my earlier suspicion that Beaumont had set the fire. Was it just as a distraction away from me being the prime? Or was it to keep people from looking too closely into Jak's actions?

I guessed that it could have been for something else entirely. Maybe the whole point was to have classes canceled. I knew that he wouldn't have had any problem getting rid of a few deltas. They were close to second-class students in the eyes of those who, like Beaumont, believed in the Old Ways.

"That's what they're telling everyone," said Cass. "One of the deltas got really hurt too. I don't know which one, though."

My heart went out to the delta that had been caught in the fire. "Do they think he's going to be okay?"

Cass's shoulders jerked in another shrug. "Honestly? I have no idea." She reached up, pressing a hand to the side of her head. "Look, this smoke is giving me a killer headache. I have to get inside for a bit." She took a step away from me. A strange look flashed in her eyes. "Be careful out here, Vic. Things are getting pretty serious."

And then she turned, and she left, leaving me alone on the grounds. My gaze turned towards the pillar of smoke in the distance. I knew that I had to figure out what was going on. And I had to do it... Fast.

28

I should have waited and talked things over more with Monty. He was my general, after all, and what he said – well, it was supposed to matter. I just couldn't bring myself to do it. Classes were canceled. Night had fallen. And from the window of my room, I could see Beaumont making his way through the courtyards and into the nearby forest.

He would be gone for a while, especially if he was going for a hunt. That meant this was a prime chance to figure out what was going on.

I left my room, and the alpha quarters.

The professors were on the next floor up from me, at the end of the hall. The Elder Alphas, at least. It was easy to find Beaumont's room. I could smell him through the door. The man's scent was unmistakable.

Picking the lock was harder than the YouTube videos made it look, but the door eventually swung open, and I was allowed to step into the room. At first glance, it looked pretty similar to my room and to Jak's room. A big, four poster bed. A dresser with a mirror. A balcony door.

But the man had brought in a lot of his own items, filling

it up with his own scent. A heavy looking black trench coat was draped over the back of an overstuffed recliner, which was in what could only have been described as a reading nook. Books were spilled over the floor around it.

I closed the door behind myself, locking it again.

The books proved to just be textbooks. If they meant something, I wouldn't have been able to tell. I still made note of what their titles were, to look up later and share with Petra and Monty.

Then I started to really root around. Nothing was hidden behind the painting by the bed, or either of the other two paintings. Nothing under the mattress, either. It struck me that Beaumont was a professor. He probably didn't think that he was in danger of anyone looking into him.

He wouldn't be hiding things the way that a student might.

So, I went to the dresser instead, pulling open each of the drawers in turn. They rattled on their hinges. Clothing in most of them, but one of them had several letters tossed in on top of the carefully folded button up shirts.

I pulled them out and gave the envelopes a sniff. A strong, acrid tang clung to the paper. Whoever had sent them had a foul odor, and a strong one.

The envelopes had been left sealed. I wouldn't be able to open them without being found out. That wasn't any help! Not now, at least.

I shoved them into the pocket of my jacket. I would go through them later.

Then I started looking through the room for that same scent. It was easy enough to find. Over in the books. One of the big leather tomes was being marked with a piece of paper. It had the same strong, acrid tang clinging to it.

Before I grabbed the book, something shining on the

end of the shelf caught my eye. It was a small, flat case with a strange triangle shaped keyhole. I picked it up, turning it over in my hands. I had never seen a keyhole like that before.

Holding it up to my nose, I gave it a sniff.

Scent blocker.

Alarm bells went off in my mind. There was no way in hell that this wasn't important.

The box was only the size of a glasses case, so I was able to shove it in my pocket, too. Then I turned back to the original task at hand.

When I opened the book, I was careful not to lose track of the pages. The paper inside was a letter – one that had actually made it out of the envelope. The writing was neat, crisp, and totally not something that I recognized.

I will be at the Academy soon. I expect you to be ready
for me.
Mikel

That was it. Two sentences and a name.

And it still managed to explain everything, the whole mystery slotting into place.

Beaumont might have been running things here at the Academy, but he wasn't running the whole show. He was working with Mikel, of House Renoir.

The question now was this: did this letter come recently, and would Renoir Prime soon be on the property? Or was the letter old, and the source of the original rumor that Mikel had been seen on campus?

Both options were nothing but bad news.

I shoved the paper back into the book, snapping the

tome shut and then tossing it onto the floor. Irritation flared inside of me. For a moment, that's all it was. Frustration that things hadn't been more easily explained. Anger that I was still missing some of the answers.

And then the frustration snapped into something else.

That same anger that gripped me when I broke Greg's jaw at my old college campus suddenly flared up inside of me. A snarl ripped through me and the power that flooded my body was so hot, it was like fire. Without thinking, I grabbed onto the chair and flung it across the room.

My muscles flexed with inhuman strength. It was the special ability of being a bear kin, and one that I hadn't made much use of. The strength, the inhuman ability to pick things up that were far, far too heavy to actually hold.

Paired with the anger, it turned me into a raging beast. I was gripped with a power that couldn't be controlled, and a fury that seemed to destroy rational thought. My only goal became to destroy as much of this room as I could.

I wanted Beaumont to know that someone was after him. That someone knew what he had done. What he was still doing.

I wanted to do *something* to make him hurt, the same way he had made me hurt. Jak's blood was still a constant tang in my mouth. I would never be able to stop hearing the way that he took that last ragged breath.

The way his breath had been warm and wet on my skin. The sound of his voice when he told me to look for the paintings. He wanted someone else to know that he hadn't done this for no reason. That someone else was involved.

That Beaumont was involved.

With a guttural snarl, I set upon the dresser, grabbing hold of it and knocking it down. It hit the floor with a massive thump. My hands came down on top of it, curled into fists. The impact caused the back of the wood to splinter.

My rage was turned onto the bookshelves. Old, expensive, and rare leather-bound books were pulled from the shelves and hurled at the wall with such strength and force, their spines snapped on impact. The bookshelf itself was the next victim of my wrath.

The bed. The mirror. The paintings.

Everything that my hands could touch, I broke. I flung, snapped, smashed, and shattered. I took as much of Beaumont's possessions as I could, and I ruined them. Broke them. Destroyed them.

And the whole time, I was tasting Jak's blood. The whole time, I was thinking about how much danger Petra was in.

By the time that I came back to my senses, my hands were bloodied with wood splinters and my knuckles were bruised. Sweat was dripping down the back of my neck, matting my hair to the sides of my face. I breathed out hard, the noise a rushed exhale, and finally moved towards the door.

I didn't bother to lock it behind me.

Fuck, I didn't even close the damn thing.

At this point, I wanted Beaumont to know that I was onto him. It was funny how quickly my decision in regards to that had changed.

By the time that I made it down onto my floor, the cuts on my hands had already begun to heal. I was busy looking over the way that the flesh was knitting itself back together when someone growled at me.

A lynx lurched from the shadows. He had been hidden using his special ability, turned into one with the darkness at the end of the hall.

"What do you want?" I demanded.

The lynx was large and scarred. But it wasn't his physical form that truly caught my attention. It was the look in his eyes. They were wild and frantic, like he had gotten hyped up on drugs before making this shift.

The lynx lunged at me. The hallway was too narrow for my beastly bear kin form. I let my body reshape into the form of a lynx instead, barely avoiding the outstretched claws of the other shifter.

He slammed into the ground at the end of the hallway, turned towards me, and snarled.

I snarled right back; the fight was on!

29

Of all the fights that I've been in recently, this one was the
least expected. I didn't know what to expect from it, or even
who this lynx was. Our bodies collided in mid-air. I
slammed myself into him, our front legs wrapping around
each other as we rolled and grappled. We broke apart, panting, and I jumped backwards.

Not quick enough.

The lynx rose up onto his hind legs. I mirrored him,
rearing up. Our paws hooked on each other's shoulders,
claws raking into thick fur. And that's when I got my first
whiff of him, and realized that, actually, I *did* know who this
lynx was.

It was Trevor.

Trevor, who had been good friends with Jak.

Trevor, who was no doubt furious that I had killed him.

A snarl ripped free from my lungs. I snapped at him,
teeth clanking noisily together. We broke apart again,
neither of us having been able to get enough leverage. The
fact that we were in the hallway meant that it was hard to
get much room for a true brawl. I tried to take off towards

the stairwell, but then stopped only a few steps in and spun around, hissing.

While my goal had been to get down the stairs and get us more room for the fight, I didn't want to do anything that Trevor might have perceived as running away. There was something definitely not right with the guy. His head was down low, and his upper lips were pulled back into a snarl that showed off not only his teeth but the mottled pink and black of his gums.

Drool was dripping down his lower jaw and had actually matted and turned his neck fur wet. But it was his eyes.

His eyes were what did it.

The way that his pupils were so blown out... There was no way that Trevor wasn't high on something. No wonder he seemed to almost be swaying where he stood, crouched down as though he was trying to stalk something. Trevor's belly nearly scraped the floor when he took a lumbering step towards me.

I snarled again, trying to use my body language to convey what I meant.

Knock it off, or you're going to regret it!

But Trevor either was too wasted to understand, or he just didn't care. He lunged forward, striking out at me. Claws brushed over my chest, but I was able to pull backwards before they could do much more than take out a few tufts of hair.

The dodge left Trevor unsteady. He hit the ground awkwardly, and I took advantage of that, bowling him over. Trevor was knocked onto his side. I threw myself on top of him, pinning him down with a big paw on the neck. My claws extended and cut into his fur, and I gave a hiss that was so mighty, it could have cut straight through glass.

Trevor snarled.

Then he whined.

And then he made the most pitiful sound that a lynx could make, this awful sort of keening slipping between his teeth. All of the fight left Trevor at once. He went limp beneath me.

My ears pinned back against my skull. The sound made my chest hurt. It made me remember the taste of Jak's blood in my mouth. I pulled back and stalked away from him. Trevor shifted into his human floor but didn't get up. He just laid there on the floor, sobbing. There was a massive bruise on his neck, and little pin pricks where my claws had pierced through his fur.

The wounds were already starting to heal.

I shifted back into my human form, too. I was sweaty and tired, but hadn't taken any hits harder than a bruise.

"He wasn't worth it," I told Trevor. "You could have done better than following around a guy like him."

"He was my best friend," Trevor sobbed, one hand coming up to press against his face. He was definitely high, and crashing hard. "You killed him!"

"He lost the fight. It could have been left at that." I shook my head. "He killed himself."

In hindsight, Jak had probably just been looking for a way to get out from underneath of Beaumont's clutches. Even death had been better than going and telling that man that he'd lost.

"I miss him," said Trevor, still not bothering to get up. "I miss him."

Nothing that I said to Trevor would have made him feel better. I found that I didn't actually have anything to say. I had made my point.

It didn't matter how sad he was. Attacking me wouldn't

bring Jak back. It wouldn't end in anything but Trevor's own defeat.

There was a part of me that wanted to go further. It burned inside of me. Hot anger that Trevor would dare to try and pull something like this against the prime alpha. But it seemed like the kind of fire that would be dangerous to give into. I swallowed hard, and this time, I did turn and head for the stairs.

I didn't kill him, but I left him lying there in the hallway to nurse his own injuries, both emotional and physical.

My glossy sneakers thumped against the steps. No one else interrupted me on the way through the building, or out through the lobby. I stepped outside and was hit with the heavy, acrid tang of smoke once more. Restless after that fight, I found that there was only one thing on my mind.

Petra.

I knew that she could make me feel better. Her peach pie smell. Her pretty smile. The way that she looked at me.

I needed that. It was the only thing that could quell the fire in my chest.

Moving through the courtyard, I tried to catch the scent of her. The smoke in the air made it hard to catch anyone's scent, though. The wind shifted suddenly, coming from behind me instead of in front of me.

Someone was there!

I twisted around, just in time to have a wolf lunge at me!

Now, I have seen plenty of lycan shifters at this point. We all had to change form during our sparring lessons and hunting lessons. But this one was different. It was the biggest lycan shifter that I had ever come across. There was something about him that just felt... Different.

It was his smell.

This wasn't just another alpha, angry and trying to make a move on the prime. This was another prime!

Fear cut through me. The only other prime alpha that would have been in the area was Mikel – and only if the rumors were true.

I staggered back a step. "Mikel?"

The name slipped out between my lips without my consent. The lycan gave an amused huff, chuffing like a canine that found something particularly funny.

His fur was pitch black, and his claws were just as dark. They were massive things, like black knives. His tail wasn't just bushy, it was also so long that it drug on the ground around him, and his fur was heavy like a perpetual winter coat. The man's upper lip curled back. There was a flash of white teeth, and then of a dark gray, almost blue tongue.

That was it, then.

This was Mikel Nazarrov, the Prime of House Renoire.

What did I know about him? Not much, as it turned out. Monty said that he was from a Russian family that took over the more European side three generations ago. He was old-blooded, ambitious, and charming in a sociopathic sort of way.

That last bit had been added on by Petra.

I couldn't see any charm in the man now, though.

A growl flooded through me. My first instinct would have been to leave but – I couldn't run.

I was a prime, and Mikel had come here for a fight.

My body twisted and shifted, pushing itself into the form that fit me best. The bear.

I was taller and larger than Mikel in this form, but he was older than I was and knew all of the tricks. Plus, I had never gone head-to-head with a lycan in anything, but a practice brawl mandated by the school. I didn't think that rolling around with Bree counted. I was always more fixated on how her curves felt beneath my hands than on trying to rip out her throat.

That seemed to be exactly what Mikel had been waiting for.

Finally, the man lunged forward. He threw himself at me, snarling. It was a sound that seemed to ripple through the very air around us. I barely avoided his hits. Those claws caught in the sun and glittered. They were deadly.

I would have to be careful. This wasn't going to be like fighting another student, who shared the same skill level as me. This was a house leader. A prime alpha. Someone that knew all of the tricks, and all of the moves.

We entered into an entanglement of limbs. I was on the defensive, my only goal being trying to get away from him and keep out from under his claws. Where was everyone else? It seemed as though the smoke must have been keeping them away. They had all gone inside trying to put distance between themselves and the tainted air.

I played the mouse – right up until my hind foot caught on something. A root, maybe. I wasn't certain. My stumble was small, but it was enough to give Mikel the advantage. He lurched forward, rising up onto his hind legs. It made him a towering thing. Then he came down, bringing both of massive paws on top of me. Claws dug into the flesh at the backs of my shoulders. It ripped my fur out in chunks.

I screamed, a wail ripping through me. The wail was loud enough that I was certain someone would have to have heard. I hit the ground chest first and rolled, swiping at Mikel's legs. I grabbed onto one of his ankles and pulled, hard. The towering lycan hit the ground.

Scrambling, I tried to pull myself back up onto my feet. Blood was soaking into my fur. The pain was intense, like nothing I had ever felt before. I couldn't rise up all the way in time.

Mikel struck me again. His massive paw slammed into the side of my face, claws cutting into my face and ripping upwards, towards my eye. It barely avoided the soft flesh of the eye itself.

I hit the ground again, wailing. My back legs struck out, kicking at him, but it was too awkward of an angle to do any real damage. The blow was more of a glancing thing. His fur got caught beneath my claws.

This was it.

The lycan loomed over me. He blocked out the sun – what bit of it was visible through the thick curls of smoke behind him. His shadow landed on me. I was in too much pain to hold the shift and dropped back into my human form. Blood ran down the curve of my face and hit my neck. It was hot. The smell of copper mixed with the acrid bitterness of the smoke.

My heart was hammering so hard in my chest that it actually hurt. I couldn't breathe through the pain. I didn't know my father, but I couldn't help wondering if this is what it must have been like for him. Was he this scared when they culled him? Had it been a friend that did it, or someone like Mikel.

I looked up at him and struggled to twist my face into one of defiance. I couldn't talk. There was too much heat in my back. The side of my face was already swelling, the skin dark and lurid in bruising.

Mikel raised his paw – and a massive bear kin slammed into him from the side, knocking him askew.

It was Monty!

There was a lynx right behind him, and I knew instantly

it was Petra. But Bree was also there, the lycan omega that I often saw in the library.

The three of them put themselves between the prime and me. The wind changed, carrying the smoke away from us. With this shift in wind, his scent would soon be all over the school.

Mikel took a single step backwards. Then he turned, and he vanished into the trees.

Petra changed back into her human form and dropped down beside me. "Victor!"

The wounds were starting to knit themselves back together, but they were serious injuries. I groaned and curled towards her, pressing my forehead against her thigh. Bree turned and ran off. Monty changed into his human form, too.

"She's going to get the nurse," he said, coming over. "Petra, is his eye-?"

There was so much blood on my face, it was impossible to tell. Petra carefully wiped it away. Each brush of her fingers sent more pain through me. And yet, it calmed me as well. She was a drug. Something that was addicting. It hurt, but it soothed me as well. I tried to press more fully into her touch.

"It's still there. Who was that?" Petra asked.

Monty shook his head. "I don't know. He looked older, but I didn't recognize him."

"Mikel," I managed to get out, between pants. "It was Mikel."

Their heads snapped towards me. Petra's voice cracked. "Mikel?"

"Yes," I hissed. "I'm sure of it."

Monty snarled. The sound came from deep in his chest. "He was trying to take out the prime alpha of House Blackstone. That's what this was all about. The smoke, Hannah, all of it!"

A wave of dizziness washed over me. I tried to press even closer to Petra's leg, opening my mouth to better breathe her in.

"He almost killed you," said Petra, a mournful whine in her throat.

Monty said, "But he didn't. Not this time."

Neither of them said anything after that. For one, the nurse and Bree were almost back, and we couldn't risk letting anyone else know what was going on, not yet. I was in too much pain to be of any help, either. The nurse dropped down, tsking over me, and pulled out something from her satchel.

My eyes slipped shut. And the last thing that I thought before passing out was this: things have just gotten a hell of a lot more complicated.

30

The next time that I woke up, I had heavy teal curtains pulled shut around me, and a white tile ceiling above me. The air reeked with the tang of antiseptic, and the burn of cleaner. And it had something else under it. The scent of my own blood, and the herbal tang of the ointment that had been applied to my face.

Groaning, I pushed myself up onto my elbows and looked around. I was on one of the cots that were set up on the far side of the infirmary. The curtains were to give me protection. I parted my mouth and tasted the air but couldn't catch anyone else's scent. It seemed as though the infirmary was empty.

I briefly took stock of my wounds. The gash on my face had already closed, though I could feel how tender it happened to be. The wounds on my back were a different story and were still in the stages of healing. They must have been mega-deep, then.

The bandages that were wrapped around them were stiff and tight against my chest. I shifted, throwing off the sheets and then swinging my legs over the edge of the bed. Outside of the bandages, the only thing that I had on was a pair of boxers.

The floor was cold against the bottoms of my bare feet. I stepped over to the curtain and pulled it back on one side, revealing the infirmary. The posters of animal anatomy on the wall seemed almost obscene for some reason, despite the fact that they hadn't bothered me before. Maybe it was just because I felt more like one of the animals than a human.

"Hello?" I called out.

The other curtain covered cubicles were indeed empty. Monty and Petra were nowhere to be seen.

I stepped out into the nurse's station and looked around. "Nurse Bellsworth?"

There was a sound from the far side of the room. A door was closed. I stepped over to the door and pulled it open, revealing a small, cozy-looking office. There was a large desk pressed against one wall, absolutely overflowing with stacks and heaps of paperwork. At the other end of the room, there was a set of black ceramic pots.

The pots contained herbs of various sorts, and flowers that were most likely used in medical concoctions.

Nurse Bellsworth was sitting behind the desk. She looked just the same as she always did, with her blouse a little on the tight side, barely containing her breasts, and her pencil skirt just a little on the sexy side. It was hitched up a little bit, showing off more of her thick thighs and the blue fur that grew there. Her blue tinged hair was pulled up into a tight bun at the back of her head, though that didn't hide her lycan ears, or the thick claws protruding from her fingertips.

"Victor!" She pushed her chair back and all but jumped to her feet. Nurse Bellsworth crossed the room, grabbed me by the shoulder, and steered me back towards the beds. "You should not be up right now!"

"I didn't know what was going on. I don't remember being brought in here." I told her.

"And your friends don't remember what happened," said Nurse Bellsworth, with the air of someone that had already grown tired of children trying to keep each other out of trouble. "I'm sure that you don't either."

My lips pursed., If I didn't want to make an enemy out of the only medical professional in the Academy, then I was going to have to give her something. "I remember being attacked by a lycan. And... By Trevor, before that."

Toss the small fry under the water and keep the big fish for myself.

Mikel had tried to kill me. He failed this time, but that didn't mean he wouldn't be back.

Nurse Bellsworth insisted that I sit back down. She said nothing as she fussed over me, uncurling the bandages, checking my wounds, and then applying a thick, cold ointment to them. The ointment smelled exactly like the herbs from her office.

Once the ointment was in place, and my skin had started to tingle, she finally put a clean set of bandages on me.

"Why haven't they healed yet?" I asked.

Nurse Bellsworth clucked her tongue. "I keep telling everyone that they need to better explain the healing process to you lot. It was important when I went to the Academy. It had its own class and everything. Now, you're lucky if it gets mentioned at all, and it's only ever in passing."

I stayed silent, just listening.

Even if she didn't answer my question, it was a good distraction from the fight. She didn't chase after answers, either. I wondered if that was because she was of such a low rank, she wouldn't have had a say in it, or such a high rank that it was beneath her.

She did explain the healing factor to me in more detail, and why some wounds scarred, and others went away.

It was all about severity. A healing factor would speed up the process, but it was just about knitting flesh and bone back together or fixing a torn muscle. The bigger the injury, the longer it took. And sometimes, the injury was so bad, it left scars.

It also couldn't fix something that was lost.

She tapped the side of my face with one claw tipped finger and said, "You're lucky that you didn't lose this eye. No healing factor could have brought it back."

"What about your magic? You have some that you use for healing, right?" I asked.

Nurse Bellsworth just chuckled, patted me on the knee, and said, "Stay in bed," before returning to her office.

I was kept there for four days. During that time, Petra came by every chance that she could. She was visiting me between classes, before them, and after. Monty came by a couple of times as well, but more to give me an update on what was going on than anything else. Classes were back in session.

A lycan delta had been killed in the fire. Her name was Samantha, but she went by Sammy. Though Monty didn't know her well, he seemed pretty broken up about it. I wondered if he happened to know someone that was a delta and was worrying about them.

The big surprise was that Bree came by.

She only stopped in once, and she looked nervous about it.

"Here." She put the papers on the desk next to me. "These are for you."

"Thanks." I flipped through them. They were notes for all of the classes that I had missed. I flashed her a smile. "I mean it."

Bree's cheeks went pink and she hurried off.

It was the most exciting thing to happen during my stay there.

I was grateful when Nurse Bellsworth let me out of the infirmary. I was even more grateful when I got to my room and found that Petra was waiting for me there. She gave me a small, almost nervous looking smile.

"I heard that you were getting out and I wanted to surprise you," said Petra.

I smiled at her, curling an arm around her waist and pulling her close. "Consider me happily surprised."

Reaching behind Petra, I opened the door. Both of my hands then settled on her hips. Kissing her, I backed her up into the bedroom and kicked the door shut behind us.

"Lock it," said Petra.

"Is something wrong?" I asked, though I was already moving to do what she asked. When I turned back around, her shirt was off, and Petra was reaching around behind her to unclip her bra, as well.

Her cheeks were bright pink. "No. I just... I wanted-"

"Oh." The word came out in a huff. I was already moving towards her, my desire snapping into existence like a rubber band pulled too taut. I was always thinking about her. Always wanting something from her.

My own lust came forward in a snap. I grabbed hold of her hips and pulled her in for a kiss that was nothing but tongue and tooth. Petra moaned into my mouth, sliding her arms up around my neck. Her fingers tangled in my hair, but there was something utterly gentle about the action. Nails scraped ever so lightly against my scalp.

With each moment that we kissed, I worked at backing her up, towards my bed. We had never made it this far before. After my defeat at the hand of Mikel, I was desperate for – something. A win. Something that was good. Something that was wholly my own.

And I found it in Petra, soft and sweet and so loving. She was mine. And I was hers.

Her back hit the bed. She laughed, a little, and then went to slide her skirt down, revealing a pair of panties that matched her bra. The fabric hit the floor. The blush was heavy on her skin now and she admitted, "I haven't actually done... This before."

"Not with anyone?" I asked her.

She shook her head. "Not unless you're counting my hand."

"I think that I'm going to treat you better than your hand," I told her, and then my hands pressed to her sides, stroking over her skin. Down, to catch on to the waistband of her panties, and then sliding them down, over her thighs. She was waxed, bare skin, and a pretty pink pussy.

The sight of it had my mouth watering. I was already hard in my slacks.

My hands kneaded at her thighs. "You're so fucking pretty."

Petra laughed and pushed herself up onto her elbows. She gave me a smile, and she asked me, "Yeah, you think so?"

"I do. You're so fucking pretty. I've wanted to do this to you for a long time." With that, I bent forward, pressed my head between her thighs, and licked up the length of her slit.

Petra moaned and tilted her head back. She made the absolute prettiest sounds while I ate her out, and she tasted just as sweet as I knew that she would. The bitter tang of her pre cum was the most amazing thing that I'd ever had in my mouth.

A hand tangled in my hair. "V-Victor!"

She was close. I pulled back, and she gave a low whine.

"That's mean," she said, breathlessly. Her hips bucked up against the air. She tried to reach for herself, but I caught her wrist and pulled it away.

I pressed her hands to the sides of her hips and held her there for a moment, then moved my hands away. Petra's hands stayed where I put them.

"I'll make you feel even better in a minute," I promised her, licking my lips. I reached up, taking off my tie and my shirt, then reaching down to do the same with my slacks. They slide over my hips. I took off my shoes and my socks, leaving the clothing in a heap.

The last thing that I pushed down were my boxers.

Petra gasped when she saw my cock, standing proudly at attention, the head a lurid share of red and already dripping. I was so turned on that it almost physically hurt, and so excited to have her – to claim her – that I couldn't half think straight.

There was a small part of me that wanted to breed her, too. To make the whole world know that she was the mate of a prime alpha.

Growling slightly, I climbed on top of her, catching her in another fierce kiss. My teeth nipped at her lower lip. My tongue curled against the inside of her mouth. I reached between us, lining the head of my cock up with her wet, spit sloppy pussy, and then slowly started to press inside.

Petra moaned open mouthed as I took her virginity, the

first cock that's ever been inside of her. She was a tight, wet heat around me. My own forehead pressed to the pillows beside her. I gritted my teeth so hard that it actually hurt, trying to resist the urge to just start fucking her hard.

"You're doing so good," I told her, breathless. My voice was a low, husky thing. "That's it, so good Petra."

I rolled my hips, pressing in harder, and then kissed her as I pulled out and snapped my hips forward. It had me fully plunged inside of her. We moaned, our voices loud and unsteady. I held my breath, struggling to try and keep still.

Instincts took over. I started to move, fucking into her. Shallow and slow at first, trying to give her time to adjust, but then so hard that it had the headboard thundering backwards against the wall. Thump, thump, thump. It thundered in time with my racing heart.

Petra was beyond words, moaning too loudly.

"That's it," I grunted. I shifted, so that I could wrap one arm around her shoulders, and drop the other between us, rubbing two fingers over the little nub that was her clit. Each time the pad of my fingers passed over her clit, her whole body jerked in response.

She was getting close. So was I – but I wanted Petra to spill first.

Just as the orgasm began to shake her body, I dropped my head down and sank my teeth into the crook of her neck in a claiming bite. Petra screamed in ecstasy, and her whole body seemed to snap tight. I could feel the shift in the world, the way that our souls were bound together.

My own orgasm was fast to follow. I came inside of her, a hot wet rush. Petra's claws scraped over the scars on the backs of my shoulders, where Mikel had injured me. Her body shook with a *second* orgasm.

In the wake of it, I stayed there, pressed against her. My lips brushed over the bite on the side of her neck. I broke skin, but it was already knitting back together. My tongue followed suit, licking the wound as though that would clear away any sting.

I stayed there, pressed against her, until I had gone soft inside of her.

Then I pulled back, slipping free. There was a gush of cum, spilling out onto the sheets. "Are you alright?"

Petra's eyes were closed. "Yeah." She reached up, pressing the tips of her fingers to her neck, where I had placed the claiming bite. "I'm absolutely perfect."

She stayed with me that night, and I took her a second time, just as slow, just as loving. My fingers on her clit. Her claws in my skin. My teeth in her neck.

Petra was mine, just as she had been meant to be. And a part of my soul had been settled in response. Those prime alpha instincts had been sated for the moment, and my own emotional cravings had, too. I genuinely loved her, and she loved me, too.

The next morning, instincts prickled at the back of my neck. It had something in me stirring. I carefully untangled myself from Petra and got dressed. She was out cold, well and truly worn from the night before. I ran my fingers through my hair, and slipped from the bedroom while I was still hooking up my tie.

The fabric settled in a loop and a knot.

It felt like something was wrong.

Not with Petra, clearly. But somewhere else.

I went in search of Monty but found him sitting out beneath one of the trees, in deep conversation with Bree and a lycan delta that I only vaguely recognized. I made a mental note to learn the names of more of the deltas. It wasn't right, that I only recognized the alphas and betas. I needed to know all of them.

That was the job of the prime alpha, right? To know and keep track of everyone in the house?

At least, that was the job as I planned on interpreting it.

So, it wasn't Monty and it wasn't Petra. It wasn't Bree either, which had me strangely relieved to know. What had me on edge, then?

I wandered through the halls of the school, trying to locate the source of my unease. That's when it hit me.

Bree might have been fine, and I was grateful for that. But... I had no idea where Cass was. I did know this, though: something was very, very wrong.

31

My search of the school turned up nothing. I was about to head back to Petra's when I realized that there was one spot that I had yet to check.

The burned delta house.

My stomach turned. It seemed like the only choice, though. If Cass was nowhere to be seen, and something truly was wrong with her... I had to know for certain, one way or another. I turned and made my way towards the building.

The air was still thick with smoke.

It burned the back of my throat and had my nose wrinkling up. It also covered up any scents in the area. That had me on edge. I knew that I could have easily found myself bumping into someone out here, caught off guard the same way that Mikel had caught me off guard.

My ears were pricked forward. My mouth was open. And I kept my eyes wide, attention on the task at hand. I wouldn't let myself be jumped, not again. That was a trend that had to be broken, and fast.

With a huff, I finally made my way to the building

itself. It was nothing but a blackened skeleton of what it had once been. The building had crumbled down, as the fire had started on the bottom floor and then spread upwards.

The lobby was charred as it could be. The upper floors had caved in and then caught fire as well. I couldn't imagine what it must have been like for the deltas trapped inside. For that poor delta girl that had been killed in it.

What would Cass have been doing out here?

I was just about to call out and see if she was truly there or not when I heard it, the soft murmur of whispered voices. Instantly, I shifted into my lynx form. Not only were my steps going to be much lighter in this form, but the special skill allowed me to merge with the shadows, slinking through the darkness, along the walls.

The ground was harsh beneath the sensitive pads of my paws. Ash stirred up with each step.

Deep into the remains of the delta house, there was Cass. And with her... It was Beaumont!

I barely bit back my angry growl before it could give away my position. Beaumont! Just the sight of him made my stomach twist and my claws come out with anger.

"This isn't right," Cass said, shaking her head. "I know that you're... You're *you*-"

"I know what's best for you," said Beaumont, reaching out and using one finger to tuck the hair behind her ear. "Pretty thing. You want a better world, don't you? A better house?"

Cass said nothing.

Beaumont continued, "This is the way to do it. The Rawlings line must end."

"Victor doesn't act anything like his father," said Cass. "He could have killed Trevor, but he didn't."

"That doesn't mean anything," said Beaumont. "Like father, like son."

It sounded as though my father had done something awful. But even worse, it sounded to me as though Beaumont was trying to get Cass to do something for him!

She looked away.

Beaumont's fingers slid down, over the curve of her cheek, and pressed against the underside of her chin, tilting it up. "Look at me, pretty one."

I hated it.

I didn't think that I had ever hated the sight of something more.

Last night, I claimed Petra as my mate and had settled something instinctive and natural within me. But now, watching Beaumont touch Cass like this, that peace was shattered. I wanted to rip off his fingers for daring to put them on Cass.

Their eyes met. Cass was frowning. I could tell that she was nervous, even though she was trying hard not to be.

"I would never lie to you," said Beaumont, firmly. "And you are being offered the chance of a lifetime. Something that any girl would want."

Again, she said nothing.

"To be mated to a prime alpha! That is an honor," said Beaumont. "And Mikel, he would like to have a pretty thing like you."

"He already has a mate," said Cass, though there wasn't much oomph in her protest. This seemed like a conversation that they had been through repeatedly, and one that she was tired of having. Beaumont was starting to wear her down.

"You are so much better than that lynx girl Jak had been eyeing up," said Beaumont. His fingers slid down from her chin, over the nape of her throat, before they pulled away.

That time, I did growl, though it seemed not to be noticed. Cass and Beaumont were so focused on each other, it was as though nothing else mattered. I loathed the sight of it. And I could smell how uncomfortable Cass was. I could see it in the look on her face.

Not to mention the fact that I knew the lynx girl in question was Petra!

So, I was right. Beaumont was working with Mikel, and he was the one twisting Jak's arm. They had wanted Petra for something, and now, they had set their eyes on Cass instead.

My nose scrunched up, ears going flat against the back of my head. All of my muscles had been pulled into a tight, unyielding coil. At any moment, that coil would snap and I would spring forward.

Cass still said nothing, though she turned her head to the side and away from Beaumont, clearly trying to get his hand off of her.

Beaumont did listen, though not without a flash of irritation on his face. He took a step backwards, and then he told her, "You have until the end of the week. After that..."

He trailed off. Cass's whole body flinched tight. After that – it was a threat. I wanted to rip out Beaumont's throat. It surprised me to realize that I felt as strongly about Cass as I did about Petra. I wanted to be closer to her. To make her mine, and to become hers. It was instinct, sure. As the prime alpha, I was born to take on mates.

But there was something more, too. Cass was a sweet girl, and I thought that she was a good friend, as well.

Certainly, she was someone that I at least wanted to get to know a little bit better.

Cass asked, a little gruffly, "Is that all?"

"Not even close," said Beaumont, but he turned and left anyway, vanishing into the other side of the ruined building.

Cass let out a heavy sigh. All of the tension snapped out of her body, and she all but curled in on herself, shoulders drooping and chin dipping down. She only stood there for a moment. Then, Cass turned and hurried through the burned delta house, going in the opposite direction of Beaumont.

She left the same way that I came in.

Though I wanted to go after Beaumont and rip him a new one, I knew that the smart thing to do would actually be going after Cass. So, reluctantly, I let Beaumont go.

For now.

Then, I turned, and I made my way through the rubble, letting both my shadow ability and my lynx form drop away. Human once more, I stepped out into the late day sun.

Cass was walking back towards the academy proper. I thought about it for a moment, and then went after her. Her ears twitched, and she stopped when she heard me thundering after her.

Cass turned towards me. "Victor? What are you doing out here?"

I shook my head, falling into stride beside her. "I was just going to ask you that." And then, to give Cass the benefit of the doubt and figure out where she truly set with all of this, I asked her, "Did you know Sam?"

She shrugged. "I knew of her. But I didn't know her." A pause. She gave me a sideways glance. "You smell like smoke."

"I think that everything smells like smoke at this point." I countered.

She hummed and we walked in silence for a bit. Right before we got to the entrance to the library, she made a sharp left and started to walk around the building. My own steps hitched in pause.

"Come on," said Cass. "Over this way. I want to talk to you."

Right. So, she was either about to tell me a lie, or she was about to tell me the truth. Either way, I would know what side of the coin Cass landed on.

With a huff out through my nose that was more animal than human, I turned and followed her. The sun was starting to set now, and the last few traces of smoke that were still clinging to the air seemed to be caught in the dusky flow of the twilight hour, turning into something fantastical all of its own.

The side of the building was well maintained. The back of it, slightly more overgrown. The building cast a shadow over us. There really wasn't anything out here, not even old cigarette butts.

The Academy grounds were meticulously cleaned by the twin maintenance men that both lived and worked on the property. They were both deltas, avians, and I hadn't spoken to them this whole time outside of a brief nod of the head.

I got the feeling that they didn't much like talking to the students that they were supposed to be cleaning up after.

As soon as we were out of sight from everyone else, she turned towards me, a frown on her face. Cass said, "I know who set Jak up."

Relief swept through me. So, she was on my side after all.

That was great.

"Do you?" I asked, still not totally willing to show my whole hand just yet. It was always best to keep something tucked away for later.

Cass nodded. She looked around, as though expecting someone to be near us, watching. I couldn't see, hear, or smell anyone else nearby. She was clearly on edge though. I waited for her to decide that it was safe to talk.

It felt like it took forever.

"I do," said Cass. "And I know why they're doing it, too."

And then – nothing.

She just stared at me.

I stared back at her. The corners of my lips pursed into a frown. I asked her, "Are you going to tell me?"

"I am," said Cass. Another long pause. She looked around once more, like she was *really* worried someone would come by. Then she said, "But I can't tell you right now."

My heart sank. "What? Why not?"

"Because it's not that easy for me," said Cass. "Before I tell you anything, I need you to do something for *me* first."

"Why?" I demanded.

Cass pursed her lips together. "Because I need help. And if I can't get it from you, I'm not going to have any choice but to get it from Beaumont."

"What do you need help with?" I questioned. Whatever it was, it must have been huge. She would never turn to someone like Beaumont and Mikel if there were any other options.

Cass reached into her pocket and pulled out a key with a triangle shaped tip.

It matched the box that I had taken from Beaumont's room.

I took a step towards her. "I need that, Cass."

Cass held it out of reach. "I want to be on your side, Victor. But there are a lot more lives at stake than just ours.

People are going to be listening here. People we think we can trust."

She took a step towards me, though the key went back into her pocket.

Cass continued, "You have to trust me when I say that I was coming to find you."

"I do," I told her. "But I don't understand why you won't just give me that key now."

A soft whine slipped from between Cass's lips. She bit it back, and turned away from me, narrowing her eyes at the ground. "Because I *know* that you're the prime. I know that. But being prime doesn't mean you're going to look out for everyone."

"I'll look out for you, Cass. I promise."

"Even if it means something might happen to Petra?" Cass said it so softly, the words felt like a burn.

I froze.

Cass's mouth pulled into a thin line. "I don't want Petra to get hurt. I don't want to get hurt either. I'm scared. And my whole family, they're at risk. I need to know that you're going to help me, help them. If you do that..."

She trailed off for a moment, then took a deep breath. It looked like Cass was steadying herself.

"If you do that," she repeated, "Then I'll give you this key. And that's going to tell you *exactly* why Mikel wants you dead so badly."

A frown crossed my face. "Because I'm the prime alpha of House Blackstone. That's why he tried to kill me earlier. If he gets rid of me, he can make a move on our house."

"It's more than that," said Cass. "Mikel doesn't just want you dead for the power. It's *personal*, Victor." A pause. "It's personal for all of us."

I wanted to say that I thought about it.

That I weighed the pros and the cons.

But the truth was, I didn't. I knew right away that the only option I had was to make this deal. I needed that key. And I needed to prove to Cass that I was different from Beaumont. I could protect her and Petra *both*.

I would make sure of it.

The End of Apex Academy Book 1

ETHAN SHAW AUTHOR

Ethan Shaw is a socially awkward Weeb that decided to finally write the handful of books he swore he would so many years ago.

I love video games, my wife, and sometimes my day job. Give me Arizona desert nights. Ube flavored anything. A new fantasy book to crack open or a nap in the afternoon sun.

For updates on future books, feel free to find me on Facebook.

HAREM LIT

To find more spicy Harem books:
Dukes of Harem
Harem Gamelit
Harem Lit
Monster Girl Fiction
SuperLit Books

Made in the USA
Monee, IL
26 October 2023

45246287R00149